LIFE WITH LARRY

LIFE WITH LARRY

An Enchanting Tale

A Novel by

Roderick A Magoon

iUniverse, Inc.

New York Lincoln Shanghai

Life with Larry
An Enchanting Tale

Copyright © 2007 by Roderick Magoon

iUniverse books may be ordered through booksellers or by contacting:

iUniverse
2021 Pine Lake Road, Suite 100
Lincoln, NE 68512
www.iuniverse.com
1-800-Authors (1-800-288-4677)

Because of the dynamic nature of the Internet, any Web addresses
or links contained in this book may have changed
since publication and may no longer be valid.

This is a work of fiction. All of the characters, names, incidents,
organizations, and dialogue in this novel are either the products of the
author's imagination or are used fictitiously.

ISBN: 978-0-595-45400-6 (pbk)
ISBN: 978-0-595-89713-1 (ebk)

Printed in the United States of America

To Mary Anne and Brian, who responded by grabbing the editing and publishing of this book 'by the horns', so this Taurus could spend more time in the Muses' pasture. I also salute the numerous family members and friends who have helped to expand and shape my experiences and my life.

CHAPTER 1

▼

Long, long ago in a Village named John O'Groats at the tip of the Scottish Highlands, a beautiful Leprechaun watched the surf dance about the rocky shore.

"What ails ya', lass?" asked her male friend.

The wind whistled through her hair, highlighting her natural charm. "'Tis a lad I met in my mind, but can never have," she moaned, sobbing into her folded arms.

"Now, now, lass. 'Tis no way for a Leprechaun to be acting. But tell me why ya' cannot have the love of yer heart. Maybe I can help. Aye, they don't call me Extraordinary for nothing."

"Well, my friend," she replied, "I don't see that it matters, because I can never have him. He's one of them—you know, a *Man*."

"Aye, 'tis no wonder you're so mournful, my dear! But you're not in as bad a predicament as ya' think."

"Why's that, now? Everyone knows Man and Leprechaun can never marry."

"To be sure. Aye … but I'm remembering something from ancient times, I am. Hmmm … *what is it, that bit o'ancient lore.…*"

After a lengthy pause, he exclaimed, "Aha … yesss, lass. I do believe there's a way."

"*A way, you say?*" she replied, her tears stopping and her face beaming like the sun itself. "Oh, do tell me at once. How can I unite with the Man of my longing?"

"'Tis a way, 'tis a way.…"

"Quit torturing me now—you must tell me before I throw myself into the very sea."

"Yer threat's idle, m'dear, and ya' know it. Leprechauns live through all eternity. But I'll tell ya' anyway, for I can't stand to see one so beautiful in the same pain I feel. Ye' see, I suffer from the very same malady."

"You *do?*" asked the lass, brushing wind-swept hair from her face. "Then why aren't you using this *Grand Secret* yourself? Is this all blarney—and you're merely teasing me now?"

"Truth is, lass, I'd as good as forgotten it since my heart's been aching for so long. Aye, 'til ya' reminded me this very moment. But do give me a moment, and I'll see if I can't recall the particulars."

The pensive pause was electric.

"Mmm … hmm.… *Yes, quite!*"

"And ya' know what, dear?" he announced triumphantly. "If ya' like, I think we can solve this heartache together for our respective loves."

"'Twould be grand indeed! You're *sure* now—for I don't want my heart set, only to be let down.... You're *certain* that we can both have our beloved Humans in the future?"

"Aye, and since ya' seem so sincere, I'll tell ya' the technique outright. Yer heart-most desire will come by great craving, untold wishing, and eternal yearning. Aye, 'til you're almost green in the face. And by such craving, wishing, and yearning, the Powers Above will allow ya' to give birth to a Human child. But there is a great price to be paid. Sadly, we can't marry our beloved, though we *can* bear their young."

"Seems like a price beyond belief. Nevertheless my friend, you've given me hope. Yes, I'll crave, wish, and yearn for all eternity if need be. For even one single moment of his love will be worth it. And bearin' his child will be Heaven."

The Extraordinary Leprechaun sat in silence as the surf danced merrily against the rocky shore.

'Aye, 'twill be my very Mission.'

CHAPTER 2

▼

Larry Leprechaun introduced himself on April 10, though I don't need the date to remember that most unusual beginning. He didn't actually introduce himself as much as he *presented* himself to me—and what a presentation!

Staring at the wall in my real estate office that day, I sat waiting for a client. It was a precious opportunity to enjoy a calm moment between the multi-task actions of showing houses and closing sales. The memory of this moment sticks in my mind because it was the last calmness I experienced for over a year.

Suddenly, a figure appeared—*pop!* and there he was. He was dressed in a smart tweed suit, rich brogue shoes, and a jaunty Scottish *tam-o'-shanter* cap. The *twinkle* in his eye caught me as much as his sudden appearance and unique outfit.

He seated himself in the client chair opposite my desk as if he owned the world.

Just as I was about to introduce myself, he vanished as suddenly as he had appeared.

My mind raced—'*Come on Johnny, you haven't been working too hard, you're not suffering from a hangover, and you've never been prone to hallucinations. You're also not over-anxious about Barry Clarke, Barbara has not been urging you to get married, and you're wide awake.*' And I remember blinking in an attempt to correct my vision.

Pop! and there he was again.

This time I shouted, "*Hologram,*" figuring that my secretary must have let the boys in to set the prank up before my arrival. The intruder smiled broadly—broader than any smile I've ever seen. And his eyes—I swear, either a troupe of fireflies was having a dancing contest or there was a field of diamonds all glistening at the same time.

Finally composed, I said, "Well sir, you really must *speak* in order to create the full effect. A *speaking hologram*—what a splendid way to enliven an otherwise dull day."

"But Mac," said the apparition, with just enough Scottish accent to make me burst into laughter, "if I'm not mistaken, holograms are only three-dimensional concentrations of light. Nothing solid."

With that, my unusual visitor rose, leaned across the desk, and extended his hand.

Naturally, I shook his hand—even squeezed it. It was every bit as solid as mine. Wincing, he withdrew his hand and sat down. Then he stared mischievously.

I'm sure what went through my mind was what every sane and sober person would have thought, '*what is this if not a hologram?*'

He vanished again with a *pop!*

This time he spoke from the empty chair, "You'll get used to it Mac. It's always hard at first."

"The name's *McMann,* Johnny McMann. And I doubt if I'll ever get used to your disappearing act—nor do I want to. Do you pull this stunt often?" After an instant of reflection, I concluded, "Ohhh, *I get it*—this is your way of softening up the realtor before making a bid."

"Not at all," replied the *twinkle*-eyed fellow. "What use do I have of property, when I own the universe?" He flickered in and out like fireflies on a dark summer evening. "But to answer the question you're not wanting to ask, Mac, the name is Larry."

"Of course. A perfect match," I answered. "The name, suit, shoes, cap, and accent—they all fit. What's next, a pot o'gold to entice me with—but pull away as you disappear again?"

"*Really,* Johnny. You've been watching too many movies, 'twould seem." We both stared, sizing each other up—though I sensed he'd done that long ago.

"Well, Larry, you're too big for a Leprechaun. I mean, you're *full-sized*."

"Would ya' rather I looked like the *Wee Folk*, then?"

"No, no. I've had enough for the moment. Are you a *Leprechaun?*"

Glancing at the intercom, I noticed that my secretary was not listening. The morning wasn't all bad.

"Not to be cryptic my friend, but the truth is that *I am* and *I'm not.* Some call us Leprechauns, but the correct term is Elemental."

I didn't know how to respond.

The grin grew wider. He playfully added, "But what's in a name, anyway? Leprechaun's as good as any."

Oh, those bewitching, twinkling eyes....

Collecting myself, I figured the search for hidden cameras and microphones would have to wait for later. For the moment, however, I decided to play this out since I couldn't figure it out.

"Okay Larry, what's next?"

"Ah, that's more like it!" he replied with a broad grin. "Well, Johnny, I've been thinking of another Experiment."

"Whoa—another? This one does seem to have pretty well played itself out.... But tell me, what are you after, anyway?"

"Ah, you're agreeable then. Well, I can promise this one will be a *real* doozey."

"A doozey, eh.... I *am* intrigued," I admitted eagerly. "And it doesn't seem I have any choice in the matter, so ... let's get on with it then—I'm expecting a client."

"I'm pleased you're with me," said the *twinkle-eyed* Leprechaun. "Watch this, then." And Larry walked through the desk. I swear—he actually walked right through that huge hunk of wood as if it had been a hologram instead of solid oak.

"Well," I said, swallowing as if the oak desk were in my throat. "I don't know how you pulled it off, unless it's part of the hologram thing. But tell me, is your Experiment to see how long I'll tolerate these pranks before throwing you out? I mean, that was a doozey, but...."

"My gracious, Johnny. I thought you'd already passed that stage. After all, Humans usually accept the reality in front of them. Since ya' shook my hand, ya' know I'm as real as yer-self—and so is the desk, right?" Larry knocked on the surface to make his point.

"But enough play acting," said the stranger. "Here's an even better Experiment—*ye'* walk through the desk." He gestured.

'Might as well get it over with,' I thought. Naturally, I banged my thigh in the attempt.

"Thanks," I growled. "So, not all your Experiments work."

"Not at all," answered the prankster. "After all, there's really no such thing as a successful or unsuccessful Experiment, is there? Just outcomes."

"Now do it again, but this time hold my hand."

Naturally, I hesitated—but then I figured that since he seemed to dissolve into the wood, maybe I could do the same with his help. This time, I found myself walking through the desk.

"*Bravo,* Johnny. Again, if ya' please."

I stepped back through the desk as if I was walking through air.

"*Splendid,*" and he let my hand drop.

"Now, to make certain," and he gestured me forth again—immediate collision.

"And now, one more time. Take my hand"—clear sailing.

"Well, there ya' have it. Ye' passed the test."

Even though my thighs ached, Larry seemed pleased with my performance. Of course, I still had no idea how all this had happened to me—a sane, sober guy with 20-20 vision.

Later, I jotted copious notes in my private journal about meeting Larry on that fateful April morning. From that moment, my journal also became known as the *Larry Log*.

CHAPTER 3

▼

The intercom buzzed. Sheila's happy voice announced, "Mr Clarke to see you, sir."

The unexpected opportunity to test this tweed-suited intruder's Elemental abilities also pleased me to no end. Inwardly, I grinned mischievously—*'let this walking, optical illusion prove himself to someone else.'*

Barry bounded into the room like the college tennis star he had been. I watched carefully to see just when Larry would vanish. If he didn't, I'd introduce him and watch how he interacted with Barry.

"Oh, you're busy," said my old friend.

"No problem," said the Leprechaun, rising—"I was on my way out anyway. Thanks Mac, and when I get things sorted out, maybe I'll take a look at the Johnson place." Turning to Barry, he continued, "By the way, I'm Larry—nice to meet ya'." With a flash of his *twinkling* eyes and a tip of his tweed *tam,* the whatever-he-was added, "I'll see m'self out, Johnny."

He danced a little jig behind Barry's back, and then vanished.

'That Leprechaun is certainly full of surprises,' I mused. *'And how did Larry know I was showing the property on Maple Street to Barry?'*

"Nice fellow," said Barry. "Even has a pleasant grip. So, he's looking at the Johnson Place, is he?"

It was good to speak with a real Human again. "Well, *Bare,* everyone thinks it's a realtor's trick to say someone else is looking at the property you're interested in. But there you have it, *straight from the realtor's mouth*—yes, Larry's interested too."

"Don't think I'm not aware that you're capable of pulling off some pretty good acts, my friend. You could have set this up beforehand."

"I'm glad you're smiling, Bare. Otherwise I might be tempted to whack you with one of your tennis racquets."

"What*ever*. But it does seem odd that he was here *just before me.*"

"So, do you want to take another look—or what?"

"No need. Pam and I really like the place. She was so enthusiastic that she asked this morning when we were going to move in. I myself can't think of any reason not to buy it, so let's make this official—shall we?" Barry paused and then added, "unless you sold it to that Larry fellow already, *that is.*"

"*Come on*—you know you're on the top of the list, even if you haven't made a deposit. Now, are you sure? I don't want you to have any regrets about this—so, speak now or forever hold your tongue."

"Let's do it. I even have my check book with me."

Never before had I made such an easy sale. So, in spite of Mr Leprechaun's shenanigans, he actually did me a favor.

Though I see in my Journal that I was still skeptical about his vanishing and walking through desks—here's what I recorded in the Larry Log that night:

> Of course everything about Larry was extraordinary. But there were no hidden cameras or speakers, the desk was real; and he shook Barry's hand, and mine as well. If it's a hoax, then Barry is in on it, too.
>
> Maybe they're both playing with my head! Still, the down payment was no fluke—Sheila deposited it this afternoon. So, we'll see whether this would-be Leprechaun shows up again—and somewhere other than my office.

That night, Barbara and I ate at Telly's on 4th Street. We had been seeing each other consistently for two years, and the relationship was looking serious. We deeply loved one another, and it just seemed a matter of making an official commitment. The evening passed quickly as we chatted, danced, and had a good time—that is, until Larry appeared.

"Why, fancy meeting ya' here, Mac," said the Leprechaun, tipping his cap. "Say, how did the real estate transaction come off …?" Switching his gaze triumphantly to Barbara and bowing slightly, he added, "Oh, so sorry—*I'm Larry.* Met yer friend at his office today."

I'm no expert in chemistry, but there was a definite *reaction* as Barb and Larry's eyes met. Perhaps they were long-lost *soul mates* or something. Anyway, they seemed so oblivious to everything around them that I wondered if this was the end of our evening ... and our relationship. It was difficult to sort out my feelings, but there was definitely something....

Larry carried on as if the evening was all about him—as if the galaxy of planets all rotated around *him*. And, if he was trying to capture Barbara's attention, he couldn't have done it more successfully. That is, until Barb caught my eye. From that moment on, she began to ignore Larry and we picked up where we left off. It struck me as rather odd how she displayed two opposing reactions to Larry in the *wink of an eye*.

After Larry left, Barbara spoke evenly. "What a delightful Man. I didn't know you knew anyone from Scotland, Johnny."

"Just met him today." I replied as nonchalantly as possible. "Now, tell me dear, did you notice anything *strange* about him?"

"Strange? No, other than he comes on a little strong. Why, is there something wrong with him?"

"Not that I know of," I lied. "He is engaging and seems quite normal. I just sense something ... but can't put my finger on it." I didn't mention seeing Larry eye Barbara's *Tom Collins,* and how the liquid mysteriously slurped itself out of the glass—she certainly didn't drink it. That little rascal even winked at me when the ice hit the bottom. Here's how it is recorded in the Larry Log:

> I've heard that Elementals don't eat and drink the same way Humans do. Apparently, they *absorb* nutrients without having to touch them. If it's true that Larry is an Elemental, and he wanted to get smashed, then the glass

should have been full after he absorbed the *Tom Collins.* Whatever Larry is, he certainly is full of tricks.

P.S. But he *did* show up somewhere other than my office!

I didn't get a chance to ask Larry about the vanishing drink for some time, nor about how 'accidental' the meeting at Telly's might have actually been. But my real estate business did continue to flourish … and I began to feel that Barbara and I should get married.

Larry had obviously been checking me out, just as I had been researching Leprechauns and Elementals. Ethereal beings don't check others out the same way we Humans do—they literally *get into their heads*. To me, that meant he'd been snooping in Barbara's Inner Self as well as mine.

"How dare you!" I yelled at the tweed-suited Leprechaun, the next time I saw him.

It was good that I did yell at him, because I found his weakness—I could literally blow him away with any sort of aggressive behavior. "What are you doing inside Barbara's head? Don't you have any Human decency?"

After adjusting his tweeds and tam-o'-shanter, Larry said flatly, "No. I do not possess one drop of *Human* decency. And frankly, what ya' think of as so noble is not at all complimentary among my kind. That's one of *yer* delusions." He puffed himself up, not caring what my reaction might be, and continued. "Now, Mac, you've aroused my curiosity, y'have. Please explain something—why do ya' call yer friend Barbara, *Barb*?"

"I don't, around you. Barb is a form of affection that is none of your business, so I save it for personal moments. Anyway, that's no concern of yours."

"Well now, Mac. Seems strange to me that ya' would show affection by naming someone after a *fish hook.*"

I was speechless. After pulling myself together, I broke into laughter.

"What I'm saying," said Larry, "is that I'm used to two Entities falling in love and becoming Committed. But they always do it with no *barbs* attached—no catches 'r hooks. They do it with love and pure devotion."

"I see," I answered abruptly, not at all enjoying the conversation with this mind-gamer. "I'm sure Elementals are free agents—*full spirits.* But I don't need to hear a lecture about the superiority of your Race, Mr Leprechaun. I only want you to get out of my fiancée's head, *and stay out.*"

"*Fiancée?* Why Mac, I didn't know you'd Committed yerself."

"Well, I haven't officially. But...."

"By the way, Mac," Larry interrupted, "I think Barb is a *ghastly* nickname. And the truth is, she's wondering right now if you're gay or are simply irresponsible."

"*What?*"

"Because ya' haven't proposed yet—after two years. She even wonders if ya' like women."

"*Larry Leprechaun!*" I growled. But after the tweed-suited one had gathered himself and straightened the tam on his head, I mellowed. "Actually, I suppose I should thank you for meddling. You did make the sale with Barry Clarke happen.

And maybe, by sticking your nose where it doesn't belong, Barb—*Barbara*—and I will actually marry sooner, rather than later."

"In that case, *all's well!* And ya' really shouldn't blast me with yer temper, Mac. It's very unbecoming, and not at all necessary. In fact, it makes me wonder if I should even honor ya' with the next Experiment."

Later, I learned that he actually wondered if I was ready for the *real* Experiment he had in mind.

CHAPTER 4

▼

There didn't seem to be any escape from this *leech-like* Leprechaun. On the other hand, maybe if I failed Larry's strange Experiments, I'd be free of it all! I wondered if ignoring him would make him go away, or if refusing to be a guinea pig might encourage Larry to pick on someone else. As it was, I felt he'd singled me out; yet I didn't have a clue as to what he was trying to accomplish or what Larry wanted of me.

In the meantime, properties sold like proverbial hotcakes—within three weeks, I closed five sales. Two were of the manor-castle class and netted enough profit to never fear a dry spell again. Several other very nice leads eventually proved to be equally promising. I suspected that Larry's intervention had helped.

But why had he singled me out?

One evening, I took Barbara to *Chelsea's-by-the-River,* the most extravagant restaurant in the city. I felt it was time to commit myself, and had even purchased a beautiful and costly engagement ring. I could never have afforded the ring without the recent sales bonanza.

Over appetizers, I fidgeted as words flew around in my mind.

"You know, Barb, we've … we've known each other for over two years, two *really amazing* years. And even though we've never … never, er…. *Oh, why is this so difficult?*"

Taking a deep breath…. "Okay, dear, let's get married, shall we?"

Without waiting for a reply, words just tumbled out of my mouth with surging joy, "I know we haven't had *sex* or anything, but I really do love you very much … and I want you to be my wife. It's just … I just wasn't ready for this before, so it's not like I'm gay or anything. I'm quite responsible, and I have a good paying job." The words trailed into silence as my mind went quiet, and body pulsed vigorously with my surging heartbeat. *"Barbara, will you marry me?"*

"Oh sweetheart … it's as if you read my mind, you silly thing," she blushingly replied, putting her hand tenderly on mine. "It certainly has been two very special years … *really wonderful* years—hasn't it? You're perfect just as you are, my dear—and you have been so caring and loving…. Yes, Johnny, I *do* love you; and yes, I *will* marry you."

I held the sparkling diamond ring out on my hand.

"But before I give you this…." I whispered.

"Oh, Johnny, what a *beautiful* ring!"

Everyone at *Chelsea's* applauded.

I felt I couldn't let the moment slip by—I had to tell her about Larry before it was too late. "Barb, we're in this together, right?"

"Of course."

"Through thick and thin, better or worse?"

"Yes dear, but something's bothering you. Let me make it easy. You can tell me *everything*—I am all yours, even if you don't have any...."

"Oh I have them, all right. It's not that—it's ... that ... I'm being *used.*"

"You're a *male prostitute?*"

"Of course not," I replied, stunned by her words. "What I mean is...."

"What *do* you mean, dear?"

"I should have mentioned this before, but was afraid you might think I'm crazy—and it's better to know everything before you commit yourself."

"Untie your tongue dear, and just tell me. You're not an *alien,* are you?" she replied with a smirk.

"You're not making it any easier, Barb. Anyway, you know that guy who stopped by our table at Telly's—when you wondered how your *Tom Collins* disappeared?"

"Yes, that charming Scottish fellow. You think he's an alcoholic, and snitched my drink?" Barbara kept looking at the diamond, so I knew she wasn't actually hearing what I said—but I had to tell her.

"Well, no *and* yes."

"Oh Johnny, now I *do* wonder if you're nuts," she giggled.

"What I mean is that he's not an alcoholic; but yes, he drank your *Collins.*"

"He couldn't have," she said, staring at the ring. "I stared at him the entire time. That is, until something snapped and I stopped studying him. Is that when he snitched my drink?"

"No. He did it right in front of you, and without even using a straw."

"Remind me to call him *Larry Houdini* the next time I see him."

"I'm serious, Barb. You see, he's not like you or me. He does things others can't."

"Like inhale drinks? I get it love, he *is* an alien."

I was exasperated. It grew worse when a drunk from the next table leaned suffocatingly close and slurred, *"Ah've seen alieenz. Ab'ducktid, too! S-studdieed us likes we wuz annimulz— enkloodin' seshull s'peer'minnz an' the hoe tin yarz. Ughhh … a-alieenz're horrrrribul…. Deyz … diz-dizgustin!"*

Obviously, I couldn't say another word, so we left.

'Bad timing Johnny, bad timing.'

CHAPTER 5

▼

Larry materialized in the back of my car a day or two later, and I wanted to stop and toss him out. "For crying out loud, don't scare me so!"

"Ha! That's for the verbal *abuse* in yer office! Besides, Mac, you're too dense to get truly scared."

"Dense—as in *dumb*?"

"No. Like physically *thick,* molecules like molasses. Don't ya' know that's why ya' can't walk through tables by yerself?"

"I wondered about that. Why you can do it *solo,* but I have to hold your hand. So, *big deal,* you're less dense."

"Not dense at all, Mac. My molecules, like all Elementals, are so spread out that we can be everywhere at once—the whole universe, even."

"Then how could I feel your hand? Barry Clarke felt it too." I was having difficulty keeping up here.

"Ye' held my hand because I'm special—we call it *Extraordinary.*"

"Aren't we all? You say that I'm *dense,* but what makes you so special?"

"I've been around a long time, I have. And age does make us wiser. But it's more than that, Mac—I'm *Developed*."

"And, not all Leprechauns are—some are more dense?"

"Most are *pure spirit*. That really means they can't even materialize, let alone shake a Man's hand."

I concentrated on the traffic.

Then Larry said, "But that's not the real question ya' want answered. Truth be known, ya' have two queries."

"If you already know what they are, why make me ask?"

"Because this way ya' can feel important. Humans need to feel important, and be in charge—far more than Leprechauns, I might add."

I almost picked off an elderly Lady at 4th Street in front of Telly's. "All right, Larry. Since you've been good and left me alone lately, I'll ask your questions. One, how could I walk through the desk by merely holding your hand, and two...."

"One at a time, Mac. Because the Law of Nature—Leprechaun Nature included—demands that things flow from areas of high density to low density—sort of like high to low pressure. So yer dense molecules disperse—spread out—when they meet my less dense ones."

"Then, why didn't I vanish like you?"

"Ye' could have, if you'd put yer attention there—but ya' focused on the table."

"Fine. So now, tell me why you're so big, if you really are a Leprechaun—not a midget like the *Wee Folk* I've heard and read about."

"I'm Special—*Highly Developed*. I knew that if I were to have my curiosity satisfied and carry out some Experiments, I shouldn't scare ya' off—not completely anyway. For that reason, I adjusted myself to a size ya' could accept. Not all Leprechauns can do that."

I wanted to park the car so I could absorb everything—or throw him out—but some force kept me going. "Well, while we're at it, how did you drink Barbara's *Tom Collins* without touching it?"

"You've already figured that one out, Mac."

"By *osmosis?*"

"Something like that."

"Then why didn't you get drunk?"

"Because I wanted to have the full flavor of all the ingredients. That doesn't mean I had to absorb the alcohol. By the way—I think yer drinks are dreadful."

"Nevertheless, *did* you get drunk?"

"Leprechauns can't get drunk. Sorry for the pun, but we're already *spirit* in form. Only physical, dense forms get drunk. But let's move on to yer question about the Experiment."

"Wait a minute, Larry. Did you have anything to do with my real estate sales? Because if you did, I wish you'd back off."

"Chatter, Mac—only *chatter*. Please, let's get down to the big one. Ask me the *biggie*."

"All right, *why did you single me out for your Experiment?*"

"Thank ya', Mac. Ye' Humans do chatter. The truth is that I opened the phone book randomly, and my finger fell on yer name."

"You sure know how to flatter a Man, *Lare*. The problem is that I don't believe you."

The Leprechaun was silent—which means that he was saying a lot that I wasn't even aware of. "Does that make you uneasy, Mr Leprechaun—bruise your ego?"

More silence.

Finally Larry said, "So, you're ready for another Experiment?"

"You'd rather dodge the bullet, eh? If you're going to *stick it to me* no matter what I think or say, we might as well get it over with. I do have a life ahead of me—you know, Barb and all." He didn't react as dramatically as when my aggressive denseness threw him against the wall, but he did wince noticeably.

"Well, sir," he finally said after some huffing, puffing, and *eye-twinkling*. "Ye' should know that ya' could float off and never pull yerself together enough to shake another Man's hand. 'Tis always a risk with Experiments, eh? And I suppose ya' could also become part of the desk, too."

"Are you giving me the choice to refuse?"

"Now Mac," said the Imp, smiling 'til his mouth looked like the Grand Canyon, and his eyes *twinkled* fit to blind the sun. "Ye' *want* to become a Wee One and visit my Land—and experience being a Leprechaun. And, for no other reason than to have something exciting to write in yer Journal, eh?"

So, that was the Big Experiment—*to see if I could break through my Human denseness and become an Elemental.* I wondered what the risks were beyond floating off into the wild blue yonder. Honestly though, Larry's brazen ploy to transform me into a Leprechaun made me feel joyful and carefree.

After all, how many people have a chance to talk to a Leprechaun, let alone actually become one?

"So Larry, you're going to shrink me—are you? Have me walk among your brothers and sisters to see if I can pass as one of them? Is that what this is all about?"

"'Tis," Larry said flatly, "for starters, anyway. And we can have a grand time doing it all, too. We can go to John O'Groats where ... ahem. And then, hop down to Inverness and...."

"Whoa!" I interjected. "We can do all that if the Experiment works, right? But if it doesn't?"

"Hopping about the land is a certainty," said the Leprechaun, obviously avoiding my question. A quick smile and he added, "I say, 'tis a certainty because I've already tested ya' on the preliminaries. Ye' know, walking through the oak desk."

"So it's certain that I can do various Leprechaun stunts, but not certain that ...?"

"Ah, how the dense do like to get right down to the bottom line."

"*Spirits* do evade issues, don't they, Mr Leprechaun? But then, nothing's going to happen to you."

"Chitter-chatter, Mac. Just answer me this—*are ya' Man enough to give it a whirl, or not?*"

"You insult my intelligence with your elementary psychology, Larry. Also, I don't like the word 'whirl'—not coming from you. Do we have to hold hands?"

"Of course."

And that was that.

CHAPTER 6

▼

Of course, I'd had my ideas about Leprechauns and their Fae-rie-land, but the actual experiences were something quite different altogether. I wondered now how anyone could convey their real-life experiences to others—because a description would be, 'it's like this' or 'it's like that'. To me, the only real way to get another to really *understand* is for them to have the same kind of experience themselves. So I wrote in my Journal—not to convince or even explain my tour of Leprechaundom, but to remind me about it in years to come.

> This Leprechaun stuff is not all it's cracked up to be. On the other hand, going from a six-foot to an *ankle-sized* Human is not a change for the meek. I was dizzy enough that I could barely stand. Larry must have thought I'd had one too many *Tom Collins*. But here's the weirdest thing: at the same time that my head swirled, I felt *free and unbounded*. And as Larry said, a Leprechaun's molecules are arranged differently, so we're bound to be more *spirit*.
>
> But the size thing is misleading—downright paradoxi-cal. I was small and huge simultaneously. Psychologically, I was bound to my Human thinking and conditioning,

yet my mind and body seemed completely *spirit*. What a contrast of opposites!

As I look at this part of the Larry Log written over a year ago, the desperate attempts to hang onto my Humanness throughout the Experiment glare at me. Of course, I shouldn't have done that. For, upon my arrival in *The Land of Whereever*, I was 'physically' a Leprechaun through and through—but only physically. The Human part—my mind— should have been left behind. Nevertheless, that is the part that stuck with me so completely that the entire Experiment was supposedly hindered—all because I simply could not surrender.

In the meantime … ahh, the Journal entry:

> Inner conflict torments me night and day. Something tells me that if I don't hold onto my *Human identity,* I might never be able to come back to it. And that's pretty scary.
>
> Leprechauns are not Munchkins—'Dwarf', 'Midget', and 'Wee Folk'—these are Human terms for them. They're … well, *Leprechauns.* Which means they look exactly like Humans, but you know at a glance they're not. When you see one, you just know that on the inside they're different.

Larry had been reading my mind, and wasn't happy. "Mac," he said stoically, "'twould've been much better if ya' hadn't written down a thing. Aye, even better if ya' hadn't even had the thoughts." Pausing dramatically, he added in a serious undertone, "'Tis possible that the Experiment might not even work because of yer doubting."

"You mean I won't be able to return to the Human world?"

"I'm sure ya' will. No, the ramifications ... they're far worse—*ya' never really left it.* Ye' see, getting small is no different than walking through a desk. But the way to see if a Human can go back and forth is to let him do it by himself—and he can only do that by letting go *completely.*"

"But if I do that, Larry, I'm afraid I may never be able to go back. Never see Barbara again. Never be *me.*"

"Humans and their egos!" Larry said without any visible sign of smile or *twinkle.*

"I'm sorry, Lare—will the Experiment be a failure now?"

"I told ya' Mac, there's no such thing as a successful or failed Experiment—only outcomes. Maybe if ya' stay long enough, yer ego'll soften up a bit and more may, perhaps ... uh, happen."

I didn't have to think long to respond. "That means that you don't give a hoot if my brains get scrambled, or if I float off to the far side of the moon."

The Leprechaun stared at the ground. "Mac, I told ya' there's risks."

My thoughts and feelings about this, authenticated by the Larry Log:

> I wish I'd gotten through to Barb—that she'd come along. If we remain Leprechauns forever, at least we'd be together. Oh, I really don't like the idea of being a Faerie Godfather *popping* in and out of Barbara's life like a mole-culeless midget!

In spite of all this, I like this little Leprechaun. I don't understand these feelings, but sense that I'll probably be able to get back this time. Just keep it together ... to-gather. *Oh, what am I saying?*

How long would Larry tolerate me? It was almost as if I were a spy, whom Leprechauns distrust completely—and for good reason. They know better than anyone the paradox that *the denser the form, the greater its ability to squelch ethereal spirit forms.* No wonder they live in remote places and vanish at the first sign of a threat. It was not comfortable knowing that as long as I remained part Human, Larry and his kind couldn't and wouldn't trust me.

"Well, Mac," Larry said, uncharacteristically down-at-the-mouth, "I'm responsible for ya' while you're here. That means ya' mustn't cause any damage—which further means ya' mustn't even *think* of violence. I suppose we might as well expose ya' to as much as we can, just in case the Experiment *works* ... that is, some outcome occurs. Now, are ya' up to a *Gathering?*"

"How should I know? I don't know what a Gathering is."

Larry laughed.

"Help me out—is it a party?—a reunion? Wise me up so I won't look foolish."

"Too late," said the Leprechaun. "But there's no sense explaining, since a Gathering is an *experience.* Be aware that if ya' show yer Human side—that dense physical thing you're so proud of—then everything'll vanish before yer very eyes. You'll also have to live with the knowledge that ya' were the cause of it all—so, just surrender into it *completely.*"

"Okay, I'll be a *good little boy,*" I promised, hoping my host wouldn't take offense.

Like a hypnotist, he snapped his fingers. And, just as quickly as Larry had *popped* up in the office, the restaurant, and the car—just as suddenly, a Gathering emerged. All the hills and valleys, the streets and roads, the treetops and house-tops, swarmed with Wee Creatures. And what a racket they made! Their laughter was so great and grand that I felt their very souls depended on the volume.

"Larry, I feel it, *I feel it!*"

"Well Mac, maybe ya' passed a *wee* test just then. Do ya' feel the bliss? I believe 'tis what Humans mean when they say, *'That's what it's all about.'*"

And indeed, it was. Every pore of my existence pulsed with pure joy, bliss, laughter and lightness. I felt like dancing and singing, howling and guffawing—all at the same time. I looked about the countless faces, knowing they were having the same kind of experience.

"Well done, lad," said Larry. "And ya' know what? Ye' didn't scare off a single Elemental with yer exuberance. Now, *that's* what being a Leprechaun 'tis all about!"

When Larry snapped his fingers, I barely felt the vertigo.

The Larry Log explains:

> Well, words alone certainly cannot bring another to feel an actual experience. For the first time in my life, I felt real happiness and spiritual freedom. No defenses, no bar-riers, just let-it-all-hang-out freedom!
>
> After that Gathering, everything I do in Leprechaun-dom will be different and more meaningful. Larry was

right after all—it was just a matter of surrendering completely. Oh, what it must be like to live in Whereever and enjoy Gatherings all the time!

CHAPTER 7

▼

Watching a Gathering dissolve certainly took getting used to. I could handle the instant *popping* into existence, but the way they all dispersed was straight out of a science fiction movie. Everyone sort of faded into a blob of laughter. I suppose my perception was altered by the experience of the Gathering itself.

"Where'd they all go, Larry?"

"Where they came from, of course. Like yerself, before it started—you're standing exactly where ya' were at the beginning, right?"

I don't know if he giggled because he was happy from the Gathering, or because he thought he'd hoodwinked me.

"This is going to take some time."

"Not really, especially since ya' already know how. Just quit trying to figure everything out—ya' *don't* have to know or understand what's happening all the time. Very Human trait, that is." The fellow's eyes *twinkled* brilliantly, and he concluded, "Just quit being so Human!"

Up to my eyes in Leprechaunness, I thought to just make the most of it. "Larry, why don't we go through the Village? Introduce me to everyone—I might as well immerse myself completely."

"That's the *spirit*, Mac. And you'll have a grand time, I guarantee. Ah now, here's a *twinkly-eyed* lass to start things off. She's a pretty one, isn't she?"

I'd never seen a Lady Leprechaun before. Did the eyes of every one of them *twinkle* so enchantingly? Fortunately, Larry did the talking, because I swear my tongue was tied in at least a double-half-hitch knot.

"How-de-do, Jenny Oliver?"

"I'm fine as always, and you know it, you rascal. But, who's your handsome friend, Mr Larry? Why, I swear we haven't seen him since John O'Groats, way back when."

I was about to ask what she meant when the *twinkle* in Larry's eyes bewitched me. "I can speak for myself, miss. *I go by Johnny McMann.*"

"You do, do you?" asked the lass. And then, with a most enchanting glance, she quipped, "And when you go *by him,* do you say 'hello' or 'goodbye'?" She laughed so merrily, I thought for certain she'd attract scores of Elementals, and another Gathering would erupt.

Had I fallen instantly in love? Larry saved me from making a fool of myself by dragging me on.

"Why so fast, Larry? I was just getting acquainted."

"Aye, but 'tis a Tour, not a stopping place. And, don't forget ya' have a Barb waiting, Mac...."

"You're not playing fair, Larry Leprechaun."

Larry looked deep in my eyes and said sternly, "I've warned ya', Mac—stop acting Human or you'll blow the whole Village away. Haven't ya' put two and two together yet—what's the opposite of a Gathering, when everyone's together and happy?"

"Well...."

"Right—being separate and sad. And believe me lad, 'tis the happiness that makes Leprechauns who they are. And sadness 'tis what makes the world of Humans fight and kill." Larry scooted me on. "Now Mac," my host whispered, "ya' saw how those Villagers became suspicious when ya' raised yer voice. So, ya' must make a promise here and now to mind yer ways. Because if ya' don't, we'll just have to call the whole Tour off."

"Interesting that first you called it an Experiment, Larry. Now, it's a *Tour*."

"'Tis because ya' haven't given it yer all, Mac. But since you're here, we should just do what we can. However, I'm afraid...."

Larry distracted me by walking into a Shop. The word that came to my mind was 'quaint'. It reminded me of a Scottish Norman Rockwell painting. Several small girls sat on the floor playing dress-up. They beamed happiness. "And where's yer mums?" asked Larry, innocently.

And, just as freely, one starry-eyed lass quipped, "Do you mean chrysanthe*mums* or our *mum*thers?"

"Why, yer Mothers, of course," laughed Larry. "And, I can see well enough that you're the *blossoms of the bouquet*, the lot of ya'!"

The girls giggled gaily. Their radiant eyes and effervescent laughter bubbled freely.

'*This is the only place to be!*'

Suddenly, three happy ladies bounced into the room. The first thing I noticed about them was that their eyes sparkled merrily. However, they didn't *twinkle* as brilliantly as Jenny Oliver's or Larry's did. And Midge, the plump one, her eyes only half-*twinkled*.

"Larry it is, and look what he's brought us," said Midge.

I knew from Larry's glance to remain silent.

"Yes, and it's a grand thing to bring such a Visitor, too," said Mary from under a broad-rimmed bonnet.

"Midge," said Penny, wiping her hands on her dough-smudged apron, "you should call your Stalwart Committed, Tory, to meet this fine gentleman." All three Mothers laughed heartily—so much that I braced myself for another Gathering, which didn't materialize. I do remember wondering which of the six children belonged to which Mother. But Larry shot me a quick reprimand telepathically, silencing all of my questions.

"'Tis not to think and wonder, Mac—that only gets ya' into trouble. 'Tis far more Leprechaun to live and experience. And, of course, be happy. Oh yes, *above all*, be happy! So don't be scaring the ladies with yer profound thoughts and embarrassing questions." It was said with enough gusto that I remembered it clearly enough to write in my Journal, '*Don't scare the Ladies!*'

As it turned out, the Tour had only just begun. Larry took me from Shop to Shop. And some things were similar everywhere—the greetings, joking, laughter, smiles, and innocence. After visiting the sixth or seventh place, I whispered, "Larry, you call these Shops? But not one of them sells or makes anything. They're more like social gathering places."

"Now Mac, ya' haven't been paying attention. Leprechauns are free souls—*spirits, remember?* And what's a *spirit* to do all day but chat and smile, and the likes? Not *do* things. That would be too...."

"Human."

"Aye. Here we chat, smile, and develop—all without barriers, burdens, or resistance. And all in order to become full Leprechauns, don't ya' see? Interested, Mac?"

"I think it's great—all the giggling and laughing, and innocent flirting. And then, the orgy of laughter and the Gatherings. Oh yes, it's all great and grand—but, is it *all* they do?"

"What more is there?" asked the Leprechaun, almost stunned by my question.

"Well...." But, I knew it wasn't right to tell him. So, I wrote down my feelings in the Larry Log after getting home. It didn't bother me that I rambled:

> Larry tells me I shouldn't *compare* Leprechauns with Humans, and I shouldn't look at them with *Human* eyes. Because Leprechauns are who they are, they don't *do* the way we do. Humans are always busy here and there—always accomplishing things. To make our relationships easier, we judge. And according to Larry, that only brings trouble. Leprechaun life may look good—all this singing and dancing and smiling—but it sure isn't the *American Way!*

A world filled with Angel-like entities flying about aimlessly, just *being?*—I don't know. Seems there's more to life than that. And, to top it all off, Larry says Leprechauns live *forever.* Perhaps I'm just too Human, too dense, to fully appreciate what it means to be a Leprechaun.

CHAPTER 8

▼

My stay in Whereever wasn't very long. After a whoozy return,
I found myself in the real estate office staring across the oak
desk at Larry. While re-acclimating, Sheila buzzed. "Are you
there, Mr McMann?"

Not fully re-oriented, I couldn't help myself. "No, Sheila,
I'm here."

Larry smiled—I knew he was thinking that even the short
Tour had done me some good.

"Well," said my secretary, joining in, "I see this could turn
into an *Abbott and Costello* routine. Because if I ask, *'Are you
here?'* you could answer 'no, I'm not *there* where you are, I'm
here where I am.'"

I chuckled.

"You have a guest, sir."

"Guest?" Usually she says 'client'. "Well, please send him
in, Sheila."

"Yes sir, though it's a *she*."

When Barbara poked her head in the door—almost to see if
it was safe to enter—Larry jumped to his feet and, tipping his

tam-o'-shanter, said quickly, "Well now, I was just leaving. I know ya' two must have a great deal to talk about with the upcoming wedding and all. And congratulations, Miss—'tis such good news, about ya' and Johnny here. Well, I must be going. Thanks for the Tour, sir."

Moving towards the door, he added, *"Good day, Barb."*

Barbara was impressed by the Imp's familiarity. Wanting to speak with him longer, she blocked his way and replied, "You've been looking at houses, then?"

Before Larry could make up any whoppers, I answered for him in all honesty, "We've seen a few."

Directing her remarks at Larry, Barbara probed, "Then, you plan on settling here?"

Ah, no wonder I love my Barb so much—she's as sharp as a tack! The *repartée* was so quick that it actually caught the Leprechaun off guard, so I helped him out. "Dear, I'm afraid Larry is not the settling kind. Yet, he has expressed an interest—right, Larry?"

"To be sure," said the Leprechaun, trying to maneuver himself out of the room. It didn't take a psychic to see that Larry felt awkward in Barbara's presence. After he finally wiggled his way out, Barbara smiled.

"Well, he's pleasant enough isn't he, dear?"

"Yes he's quite a guy," I agreed and hugged my fiancée. "What brings you to the office?"

"I know you don't want me barging in, dear, but I just had to tell you that Tammy and I picked out the wedding dress this morning. Oh darling, look—here's a picture."

"Tammy and you … hmmm … pretty dress. It's really nice—I like it."

"Good. Tammy's going to be my Maid of Honor."

"Of course. She's your best friend."

"Which reminds me, Johnny-dear. Have you decided who will be your Best Man?"

"Larry," I blurted without thinking—*'why in the world did I say that?'*

"Really? *Not Barry?* You've known Larry for such a short time.…"

"Longer than you think, Barb."—*'Where are these words coming from, anyway?'*

My fiancée stood silently. Then, eyeing me closely, she asked, "Are you okay, dear—you look as if you could use some rest? How long was your Tour with Larry, anyway?"

"Yes. Uhh … no and not long."

"Begging your pardon …?"

"Uhh, I'm okay Barb. What was meant is … yes I feel fine—and no I don't need rest. And, the Tour.…"

"Aha.… You're in one of your playful moods—the 'I'm here' routine with Sheila. Okay, it's Larry then. Is it L-a-u-r-e-n-c-e or L-a-w-r-e-n-c-e? Must get the spelling right for the invitations and program. By the way, what's Larry's last name, dear?"

She had me there. All I could say was, "Larry's a Leprechaun."

'Is Larry controlling my brain? Larry, please stick to your own conversations!'

"Lawrence A Lepricorn," she announced. "Fine, one less thing to do. Now, about the announcements."

If I'd tied my sweet fiancée to a chair, duct-taped her mouth, and glued her eyes lids open—even then, I don't think it would've been possible to completely command her attention. *Are all women like this before the big day?* But having told her about Larry, I was off the hook and no longer felt guilty. If she couldn't *hear* or *understand* what was said, well that was another thing.

Every time I read my Journal of that day, it brings a smile and a chuckle. How the most unusual beings and experiences kept *popping* into my life! Admittedly, I really got sucked into all of the happiness and *spirit*-stuff, enjoying it immensely.

> Well, Larry Log, this experience was a real doozey! I went to a real Leprechaun Village—named Whereever, no less—with a VIP Wee Folk as a guide. There was a joyful Gathering, and I met the single most *sprightly* Leprechaun named Jenny Oliver. Also talked with some Lady Leprechauns with six children between them, then *popped* back into this reality faster than the *wink of an eye*. Maybe I should burn this Journal before someone thinks its author is *truly* bonkers? Hmmm....

The next few days were a bit of a blur, and my memory rather fuzzy from all the extra activity. I was all ears when focusing on Barbara's busybody pre-marriage excitement. At other times, I confess that Leprechauns would frequently be foremost in my mind—wondering about Whereever, and whether Larry would ever invite me to attempt the full Experiment.

Numerous doubts about Larry's Experiment remained. After all, I'd 'cheated' the first time by not actually letting go of my Humanness completely—and *after* agreeing with Larry to do exactly what he asked of me. Namely let go and surrender completely. I held back and *couldn't* let go—it would be like *dying*, or so it seemed. Anyway, until certain of my ability to surrender completely, there was a strong possibility of never seeing Larry again.

This presented a real problem. I had told Barbara that Larry would be my *Best Man*. So, if he didn't show, there'd be big trouble—imagine standing at the altar with no Best Man! 'It's all right, dear,' I'd explain, 'lot's of weddings happen with last-minute substitutes, right?' … 'Maybe he got caught in traffic or had a wreck.'

It also occurred to me that if Larry showed up before the ceremony, I might not even want him there. After all, he hadn't even been invited to stand with me at the altar as my Best Man—and we could even get into a verbal duel.

Larry's explanation about picking me randomly out of the phone book for his Experiment still bothered me. And that ruddy Leprechaun even had the nerve to *pop* into my office and march me through my desk, without as much as a *would-you-mind?*

All said and done, it seemed uncertain whether I'd ever see Larry again.

CHAPTER 9

▼

But, I did see Larry again—the night before the wedding, and as if on cue. Larry's arrival was as much of a surprise as how happy the Imp appeared to be—and he didn't seem to be putting on an act. I was pleased that he had accepted our marriage, and the honor of being my Best Man.

"Bit humorous, isn't it, Mac—Best *Man*? If they only knew!"

"They do know, Larry."

"What?"

"Well, Barbara anyway. I told her the day we returned from the Tour."

"Really? And how'd she take it?"

"Like water off a duck's back."

"You'll have to translate that one, Mac."

"All right, the news went in one ear and out the other."

"You're just full of *clichés* today. Is that a Human wedding-day tradition? Can't ya' just state clearly how yer fiancée received the news that I'm a Leprechaun?"

"Of course, Larry. It didn't register one iota."

"Just a wee bit more concrete and I may be able to understand ya'."

"Okay. When I told Barbara straight to her face, she didn't hear a word. She was thinking about the wedding, wedding gown, and invitations. Even when your name was spelled out, she didn't react. By the way, I hope you don't mind that you are now Mr Lawrence A Lepricorn."

Larry smiled his *Cheshire Cat* look, complete with *twinkling* eyes.

"That amuses you?"

"Not really. I'm smiling because I'm happy—'tis what Lepricorns do, ya' know."

"You're not mad about my telling Barbara?"

"You're entirely too serious, Mac," laughed the Imp. "Ye' forget that being happy and Committed are the most important things to Wee Folk. Well, that and maintaining the *twinkle*. 'Tis most gratifying to know you're not going to bounce from one sweet lass to the next. You're *Committed,* and no longer fishing."

"Oh," I said, jumping ahead. "Does that mean you've decided to use both of us in your next Experiment? Is that the real reason you showed up?"

"You're getting good, Johnny. Now, don't fret over anything—'tis yer *big day,* too. And, I'm sure Barbara will enjoy it all the more with ya' more relaxed. Aye, I can sense it."

"More evasion. By the way, why Barbara and not *Barb*? You don't consider her a *thing* anymore, part of a fish hook?"

"Some women," began my Best-Leprechaun, "seem to like fishing for sport. Ye' know, catch this one and throw it away, catch another.… By getting married, Barbara has shown that she's no longer fishing either. She has made a definite Commitment—so the *barb* has disappeared."

"It gratifies me that you have accepted her, Larry."

"Well said, Mac. Now, ya' have only to convince yer new wife to accept the Experiment, because I wouldn't think of taking ya' alone."

CHAPTER 10

▼

I might have enjoyed my honeymoon even more, had Larry not mentioned the two of us joining the Experiment. But, what can a Man do who knows a ubiquitous Leprechaun, one who might just *pop* in at any moment and say, *'Let's go!'*— That Leprechaun was certainly full of surprises.

Mrs Johnathan B McMann was still unaware of the Imp's true identity, even though Larry had accepted the once-Barb for the Experiment. My anxiety about her accepting Larry-the-Leprechaun and his Experiment made me feel like I was sitting on *pins and needles*.

From my bad timing at *Chelsea's,* I'd learned to wait for the right moment to spring the news about Larry. Sure enough, the propitious time eventually presented itself when we were 'as snug as two bugs in a rug,' and didn't have a care in the world. No defenses—just open to everything. I smiled when Barbara said, "Let's trade secrets".

"Sure. But … ladies first, beauty before age, and all that."

"Okay, dear. Here goes … uhh … er … well, I saw an Angel."

"Really?"

"I wouldn't have said it if it wasn't true."

This news thrilled me, and was great by itself. But it also made it easier to tell her about Larry. "What was it like? Did she speak? Wait—maybe it wasn't a *she*. Barb, tell me all about it."

"I will—but you seem more curious than surprised. Why's that?"

"Because you're such an Angel yourself. So, it's only natural that one should visit you."

"*You!*" She tickled me, and then continued. "Well, I didn't really see her face, and she didn't speak. But if she wasn't an Angel, she was the next best thing. Oh dear, I was afraid you wouldn't believe me."

"Oh, I believe you all right, Barb. But tell me, did she fly around—vanish—walk through a desk? And what could possibly be the next best thing to an Angel?"

"More and more questions!" she rolled her eyes as she replied.

"Hey, it's not every day that your wife tells you she's seen an Angel."

"Well, I couldn't tell *exactly* if she was divine or not. You see, she wasn't really all there."

"Then she wasn't the stereotypic, gossamer-winged glowing Angel?"

"No. In fact, she was somewhat plump. And mildly awkward—almost bumped into things. I felt this might have been the first time she'd shown herself."

"Did her awkwardness amuse or confuse you?"

"Why, you *are* full of questions! Well, I was so taken by the experience that I just watched, and might not have caught everything."

"Just one more little question, dear. Did she *do anything* that suggested she really was an Angel?"

"*Now you doubt me....*" Barbara complained, her words trailing off accusingly.

"Well, she disappeared ... and then re-appeared. Yes, there was one more thing.... Though I couldn't see her face perfectly, her eyes did seem to sort of *twinkle*—and that really stood out. Anyway, would you believe when I sneezed, it threw her across the room? The plump little Angel ended up flattened against the wall, and that's when she disappeared for good."

"Wow. That's a glorious ... marvelous experience, Barb. Thanks for telling me."

"So, now it's your turn. What secret are you going to reveal to me?"

"You'll see. But just in case, you might brace yourself."

"Ooh, sounds good—but remember, it must be true. And, in order to be a real secret, you must never have told it to anyone else."

"Well, that blows that. I've already told someone."

"*Who?* Who would you tell the deepest secret of your entire life to, but your very own wife?"

"Ah, you guessed it—I've already told you."

"Huh? If it was a big secret, then I should have *oohed* and *aahed*—and I don't remember doing that."

"Oh, you did *ooh* and *aah,* but over your wedding preparations, not the secret."

"Dear, just when did you tell me?"

"*At the office*—and it taught me not to tell you things when you have something else on your mind."

"Sorry, Johnny—but I'm all ears now. So tell me, and it'll be like the first time."

"You're sure you're not thinking about writing *thank-you notes* for the gifts, telling Tammy and your friends how great the honeymoon is, and...."

"*I promise.*"

But, the magic of the moment had disappeared with all of the questions. My revelation would certainly have been anti-climactic. So, I handed her my Journal instead.

"It's all in there," I said, rolling over.

As she read, the strange feeling came over me that someone was watching. And you can bet your brogues that I knew who that someone was—Larry Leprechaun, aka Lepricorn.

'Have a little decency, Larry Leprechaun! Honeymoons are sacred for two people only. Would you please move your ethereal non-body out of here, now!'

Even though I felt the invisible Leprechaun presence leave, it was a tense moment. Barbara had to know the truth, and Larry would have to accept it. And, if she didn't embrace Larry's existence and my visit to Whereever, then Larry would have to try his Experiment on someone else.

The funny thing is that I actually wanted to be Larry's guinea pig. It was even a surprise to me to find myself as curious as the Leprechaun to know if a dense Human, having completely surrendered to becoming a Leprechaun, could return to his Human form after experiencing Leprechaunness.

I also wanted to hear Barbara's verdict after she finished reading. So she continued to read, undisturbed.

CHAPTER 11

▼

Barbara's reaction took me by surprise. Instead of saying, 'What a fantastic story, Johnny—I believe everything,' or 'Larry is going to have to walk *me* through a desk, before I'll believe any of this,' my wife eyed me intently.

"If this Jenny Oliver is so utterly enchanting and endearing, why didn't you Commit yourself to *her* on the spot?"

I wasn't ready for that reaction at all—"*Huh?* Aren't you going to comment on the secret—about meeting a Leprechaun and going with him on a Tour of his Land?"

"Oh … that …" she answered, as if it was nothing.

"*Barb …!*" I pleaded—but then it hit me that women certainly know how to set their hooks into a Man, barbs and all. *'Why, Larry Leprechaun, you saw this coming!'*

And then, her sudden about-face surprised me yet again— "It's all right, Johnny. By marrying me, you have made a *real* Commitment. All the Jennies in this world or any other mean nothing, right? Now it's you and me forever—that girl's just someone from your past."

Now, *that's* the reaction I'd hoped for. Nothing at all to gain from bringing up more details about Jenny—even those urgent little nudges in my brain about having only met her once, and only having said 'hi'.

"So, my darling husband, or Committed, or whatever you prefer—when do we meet our charming host and set out for Whereever?"

Yes, I married the right woman after all.

CHAPTER 12

▼

"Now dear," Barbara said before Larry *popped* in again. "I know you've thought of no longer writing in your Journal, and even throwing out the old entries. Please don't—that would be such a loss!"

"How so, Barb?"

"Because our great-grandchildren wouldn't be able to say their great-grandparents knew a Leprechaun, and had proof with dated Journal entries ... maybe even pictures."

"Don't know about the picture idea—I have a feeling Leprechauns are too shy for that. Anyway, they might not even show up—the Wee Folk are mostly *spirit*, you see."

"Nevertheless, you really should continue writing in your Journal. And include as much detail as possible."

"Why detail?"

"To better document our experiences, love. And what a document it'll be—for one thing, proof that Leprechauns really do exist! Even if we can't take pictures of them ... well, thirty or forty years from now, we can look back and re-live all the time spent with them. Doesn't that sound *exciting?*"

"Everything my dear wife says sounds good. Now, if Larry will only show up."

Larry did show, but only at the very end of our honeymoon. He *popped in* right on cue—just as he had before the wedding.

What a talent, knowing just when to show up

"Larry," said Barbara, "I'm so happy you're here!" Then, she did something completely contrary to Leprechaun etiquette, and it must have shocked him—she gave him a great big warm hug.

Fiddling with his tam-o'-shanter, Larry stammered, "Why … Mrs McMann … Madam … I.…"

"No more of this hemming and hawing, Larry Lepricorn—no more testing. Let's just get down to business—*the full Experiment*. Tell us what we need to know. You know, the ground rules."

Shy by nature, Leprechauns prefer to sneak in the back door rather than crash through the front. And, though Larry was an Extraordinary Imp, Barbara's very intense Human greeting must have seemed like a veritable gale. I could actually see him leaning forward to stay upright against that powerful force.

"My … *goodness!*" sputtered the Elemental. "Well, the first thing to remember is that ya' must not come on too strong, especially when greeting a Leprechaun. Ye' see, we're a bit fragile, we are. Aye, we'd rather size up a situation before committing ourselves. Kind of like—as ya' Humans say, 'sticking yer toes in the loch to check the temp before jumping in'."

"I understand," said Barbara, landing a kiss on the Leprechaun's cheek. "And thank you for the advice. Are there any other common practices we should know, so we won't look too foolish while visiting Whereever?"

Larry was noticeably discomfited. He'd just told my wife to ease off, when she immediately sent another emotional blast fit to sink a battleship. As I watched him react, it occurred to me why he'd made a point of her nickname 'Barb' earlier. My sweet wife had a way of *catching* everyone she came in contact with—not just me.

'Is Larry reconsidering using us for the Experiment because of her?' my mind inquired.

I jumped in to minimize the awkwardness—"Please help us out, Larry. We don't want to upset any of your plans."

Larry was silent. His smile wasn't nearly as big as the Grand Canyon anymore, and his *twinkle* no longer challenged the sun. This could well have been the most trying moment of our relationship. Finally Larry spoke, but so fast that I didn't even try to catch it all—hoping everything he said would simply be absorbed.

> "Leprechauns are shy—We never sleep—We eat and drink by absorbing like when I drank yer Tom Collins without touching it—We don't go to the bathroom—You're ninety-nine point nine-nine-nine percent spirit at yer best—Whatever we put our attention on we can do or become—Dogs can't bite us only our pants—We can sing and dance forever—Happiness is our byword—We're Curious—We like to watch—We don't pass judgment—We can become invisible at will—We can live anywhere but we prefer

remote areas because there's not as much threat from Humans since they're so violent—A Gathering is one of our Greatest Joys although number one is twinkling—Souls are born but never die—You'll be accepted as newborns in Whereever—Leprechauns hid after the last Human Invasion because we feel hurt in the heart whenever there's a threat— We disappear—Sex is unnecessary among Leprechauns— Our young emerge out of pure Leprechaunness and Committ-ment—We just be with our Committed and forever too— Are there any questions—Good."

Barbara and I looked at each other and broke into laughter.

To which Larry responded, *"We also don't like to be made fools of or humiliated in any way—Especially by Humans— Thank ya'."*

That stopped us short—all we could do was be silent and wait.

"Good," Larry continued, speaking normally. "So now ya' know that the bottom line behavior of all Elementals is, *'when in doubt, smile and do nothing.'"*

Barbara beamed—and without being too forward, said, "Thank you, Larry. I could never have remembered all those rules anyway!"

I was proud of Barb's boldness and ability to learn fast, but not at all certain how Larry felt.

At a slightly lower volume than her first attempt, my wife said, "Well, Mr Lepricorn, the *Big Experiment*—shall we?"

Obviously, this wasn't going to be as easy as Larry had thought. He hesitated long enough to let us know this was *his* Experiment, and *he* would call the shots.

The pause was impregnated with an inexplicable feeling—*coming from Larry?* I felt something distant, something faint struggling to reach the surface: '*... the subtle splashing of waves on a shore ... a desire ... a wish ... something begun long ago that would still take time to consummate ... love ... but now resistance ... be patient ... things aren't always as they seem ... yes, be patient....*'

Larry broke my train of thought by speaking. "If you're ready, I am."

With that, Barbara held the Leprechaun's left hand, and I the right. We vanished and went into the cloud that had made me whoozy on the first tour of Whereever. This time, however, the transition was smoother; yet I wondered how Barbara was taking it.

She answered the concern when she exclaimed, "*Wow, wasn't that a wild trip!* Now tell us, Larry, what are the rules concerning this Experiment?"

But it was too late—*it had already begun.*

CHAPTER 13

▼

Oddly, Whereever felt like home—the seat of my very heart and soul. Returning here seemed like returning to the womb. It was certainly more than mere familiarity—seeing the familiar Shops, the smiles, and the carefree attitudes everywhere. Why had I been gone so long?

Naturally, I was very interested in how Barbara would like Whereever, and how the Villagers would accept her. And some part of me secretly wanted to know how well Barbara and Jenny Oliver would get along, especially after Barb read my Journal.

'Strange that Jenny would come to mind at this moment.'

At the same time, the fact that I wanted to see Jenny and *not* see her intrigued me. As it turned out, the first person we met was not Jenny, but plump Midge of the Three-Mothers' Shop.

"Good to see you again," said the Mother of how-many-no-one-knew. I smiled, happy to see her too. It hadn't occurred to me that she might also be speaking to my wife. But Barbara picked up on it and spoke accordingly, "yes, it's good to see you again dear. You seem somewhat familiar, but just where did we meet the first time?"

"Why, in your own bedroom. You don't remember how you stared, not quite sure if I was an Angel or a figment of your imagination? And, to be sure, your sneeze nearly did me in."

"Oh, that was *you!* Yes, yes—it's so nice to see you again, and this time completely."

I trusted Barbara would have the good sense not to blow the *spirit-lass* away again. With that fear dispelled, the conversation began to be amusing. Until then, Larry had been the only Leprechaun I'd seen materialize. It made me wonder just how many Elementals walk about the earth unnoticed.

The rest of the day we spent being introduced in nearly every Shop in the Land of Whereever. And such greetings, smiles, happiness, and the joy of hearing, "Here's another one, and she's Committed as well! Isn't she a joy?" Throughout the day, I distinctly felt that her presence and acceptance were not accidents. In fact, Barbara fit in so perfectly that she probably would have been chosen to join the Experiment even without me.

And then Jenny Oliver sauntered over.

To my relief, the meeting was more than friendly—it was downright amiable. Barbara and Jenny behaved as if they were sisters. They even seemed to ignore me after the greeting, which was more than a *how-dee-doo*. It went more like, "Hello there, Johnny McMann. How grand that you've Committed yourself since we last spoke." Turning to Barbara, she continued, "'Tis a grand thing, Madam, that you've made an honest

Man out of your Johnny. I thank you on behalf of all the Villagers for joining our ranks."

Jenny's eyes only sparkled at first, but changed to a *full twinkle* as the conversation progressed. After awhile, a distant and faint sensation bubbled within my feelings, much what I'd experienced before: '*... waves splashing ... long hair flying in the breeze ... desire ... wish ... eventual fulfillment ... but patience is needed....*'

Later, Barbara said, "What a fine lady, that Jenny Oliver. No wonder you were so taken by her, dear."

"A fine lass she is, but I wasn't really *taken* by her, dear—only impressed by how happy and joyful she seemed to be, just like all other Whereever residents." For some reason, I did not include Jenny in that night's Journal entry.

"Where else did you and Larry go on your first Tour, Johnny?" asked Barbara. "I'll experience everything in time, but this is so exciting that I'd like to see it all now."

"Not sure exactly where to begin," I answered.

Barbara thought for a moment and said, "In your Journal, I believe that you wrote about going to a Gathering."

She looked at our host and asked him, "Larry dear, can we go to a Gathering?"

Larry smiled. "Ye' should know, Mrs McMann, ya' don't *go* to a Gathering. They just happen."

"Aha, so it is.... Well, what prompts them? If we know what triggers one, can't we just do *whatever,* and one will happen?"

"No such luck," responded the Leprechaun. "It's more like reaching a threshold of happiness. And then, *pop!*—it happens all by itself."

Somehow that didn't ring true to me.

"Well then," said Barbara, "let's *pop!*—because I'm feeling such *awesome* happiness that we could surely raise the Gathering all by ourselves."

Larry was so pleased that he smiled his famous wide grin. But he spoke moderately, trying to restrain himself while intending to calm Barbara's exuberance. "Just so ya' know," said the Imp, "I repeat—*'Gatherings don't happen by mere desire.'* That is, not for the ordinary Elemental."

"Well, Johnny tells me that you're an *Extraordinary* Leprechaun. So why can't you just snap your fingers and make it happen?"

The Leprechaun burst into such a guffaw that everyone looked up. And to my surprise, his joy triggered off the very thing my dear Committed had hoped for.

Hundreds, thousands—oh, the entire landscape was peppered with so many Leprechauns that a super-computer couldn't have totaled them in an hour! And all so happy, so *twinkle-eyed*, so full of song and dance and laughter and joy! I beamed ecstatically, and then noticed that Barbara's face had miraculously transformed, and her eyes *sparkled more than they ever had before.*

Larry was always aware of everything, and took particular notice of my wife's eyes and state of euphoria. Oddly, I'm convinced that this Gathering lasted far longer, and with much greater intensity, than my first one.

Later, Barbara summed it up by saying innocently, *"That was like a honeymoon in Heaven."*

CHAPTER 14

▼

It turned out that Larry was more than an Exceptional or even Extraordinary Leprechaun—he was also a *Recruiter*. And Midge, the plump and sweet Mother who'd visited Barbara in her bedroom, was one of his apprentices. That is why her visit to Barbara was only partially successful—Midge was still a neophyte. Perhaps with a little more tutoring, she would be able to dematerialize and materialize completely at will. As Larry was finding out, recruiting and adeptness didn't happen overnight.

Larry was not the only Recruiter. I learned quite by accident that there was one Recruiter for each continent: Bascomb's Village near Vienna, Lung Chu's in Nepal, Pauul's in the Congo, Julio's occupied Uberlandia in South America, Sidje's resided directly on the North Pole, Ooma's directly on the South Pole, and Prize Recruiter Brian's was the Australian Outback. Surprisingly, there were no Extraordinary Leprechauns in the British Isles, though Bascomb covered all of Europe and sometimes resided there. Larry covered North

America. I never understood why Larry, who dressed in all-Scottish attire, didn't oversee Europe.

It came as no surprise that Larry, and all Elementals in general, dislike boundaries—it must be due to their *spirit* nature. But our host did *sneer* every time the idea of selling a plot of land as real estate was mentioned—"Ye' buy and sell land? I don't understand—how can ya' sell it when ya' don't own it, and never can? Land is like air—or space. No one can own the likes."

After he thought a moment, he amended his statements, "Ahh, it's because you're Human—*you're dense.* The mere species is bound by its physicality, so it stands to reason that ya' would think land can be owned. But while you're at Whereever...."

"Not to worry, Larry. We have a saying, 'when in Rome, do as the Romans do.' I wouldn't even *think* of selling property in Whereever!"

Larry sighed in relief.

Because of their dislike for boundaries, Elementals inhabit regions only *approximately*. Bascomb, for instance, lived near Vienna; but also stayed in Portugal, Greece, Ireland, and Wales. The same with Lung Chu, who was sometimes in Korea, occasionally in Mongolia, and frequently in the steppes of Russia. While Leprechauns are not nomads, they certainly seem to like moving about—or having a change of scenery once in awhile.

After learning about the locations of the major groups of Leprechauns, I peppered Larry with questions—so many questions, in fact, that he seemed on the verge of being judgmental. "Ye' learn these things by experience, Mac. Be around a millennium or so, and you'll pick up everything effortlessly. May I suggest that ya' shelve yer Humanness, yer desire to know everything right now—and just *be*?"

Before he clammed up or pulled one of his vanishing acts to avoid answering, I managed to pick his brain enough to make several Journal entries. There was so much information that I even considered publishing the Log, but Barbara said that would be a direct violation of the Leprechaun's compulsive need to remain unknown to Humans. Nevertheless, my fellow *'sapiens* would probably find much of it rather fascinating.

Each Recruiter's job was to bring into the Leprechaun fold those Humans deemed worthy of sharing the *spirit* world with like-minded beings. Hearing that, and knowing that Midge had already visited Barbara, I knew intuitively that Larry would accept Barb for the Experiment. After all, it was Midge's report that convinced him that Barbara was, as she called it, *ripe.*

Curiously, the Recruiter's job is so unique that it can only be done by an *Extraordinary* Leprechaun. And the Recruiters apparently believe that Humans are the only ones capable of crossing the threshold from the dense Human body to the *spirit*-dominated being of Leprechaunhood. It suddenly occurred to me why Larry kept calling the undertaking an *Experiment*—one did not attain Leprechaunhood by the opinion of a Recruiter or consensus of any group. Leprechaunhood can only be attained by reaching a very high level of development.

Walking through the desk with Larry proved that I had reached a decent level. Not blowing the Wee Folk away while at the Gathering or in the Village were also favorable signs. I got low marks, however, by not surrendering completely during my first visit to Whereever. It would be interesting to know what score Barbara racked up when she sneezed and flattened plump Midge against her bedroom wall. As well as when Barbara came on so strongly in accosting Larry about going to Whereever!

When Barbara and I realized the Recruiters' ways—and how one changes from Human to Leprechaun—we wondered why either of us were being given a second chance. Maybe Larry thought we had promise. Or perhaps there was something in Larry's plans we didn't know about? We certainly didn't consider ourselves *shoo-ins.* Obviously, our Leprechaun-future depended on reaching and maintaining a high percentage of *spirit,* as close to one hundred percent as possible.

CHAPTER 15

▼

The *Whereever* name for these Leprechaun Villages came as no big surprise to me, because of how ethereal everything 'Leprechaun' tended to be—although they could just as easily have been called *Whenever, Whatever, Whyever, or Whichever.* Anyway, our Village was directly in the *twilight zone* between earthy physical existence and Leprechaun Land—a conclusion I didn't have to reach myself, since I once overheard the Recruiters when they gathered for a conference. But why did they even meet, since most of their communication was normally done telepathically?

Was I *meant* to overhear their conversation? At the time, I wished that my Journal was not resting on the bureau back home. Oh, the Larry Log would have been much more complete, and it would have also helped me remember more of what I heard. But, this is my summary:

> Whereever Centers seem to function as 'middle zones'.
> These are the places where newcomers prove themselves.
> We, as the most recent apprentices—and not being
> full-fledged Leprechauns—were still too Human to live in

pure Leprechaundom. If our actions here, where density was far greater than in the Land of the Pure, could blow away the Wee Folk—then our mere presence in Leprechaundom would certainly cause havoc, if not downright destruction.

Not everyone at Whereever was a recruit. There were some real Leprechauns other than Larry. Their job was to set an example for the neophytes. My guess is that Jenny Oliver is one hundred percent Leprechaun—aye, with those *twinkling* eyes she could be nothing else. Since it wasn't obvious who else was an Elemental, it became a pleasant guessing game. Maybe Mary and Penny, joint Mothers with Midge—they could easily have been pure Leprechauns helping their Shopmates develop. But it didn't really matter who was and who wasn't—the underlying purpose was to create full-fledged Leprechauns.

One of the first things Barbara and I did after our initial Tour, was to set up our own Shop in Whereever—more accurately described as a *Non-Shop*. None were businesses, unless you spelled them *busy-nesses*. Had they been in the physical world, their purpose certainly would have been to produce or sell goods and services. In our Whereever Village, however, these Shops seemed like nothing more than social stopovers. Each Shop resembled a worldly Human business according to its Shop-Keepers. Ours was half real estate office and half kindergarten—complete with playground, since Barbara was a teacher.

No Shop was occupied by a single individual—nor even a twosome. Several Non-Committeds would claim a Shop, while more than one couple always resided in another. Since

Barbara and I were married, we shared with two other couples—Mike and Sally McGee and Sean and Sarah Lowrey. Regretfully, I never figured out exactly who was a Leprechaun while in Whereever, nor who was a recruit like ourselves. The reason for this is that Leprechauns have the uncanny ability to *un-twinkle* their eyes at will. It was a defense mechanism they'd learned eons before to protect themselves. I found it rather amusing that anyone would want to camouflage their true identity while at Whereever. At any rate, not one of our four Shopmates ever *twinkled* their eyes in our presence.

Mike McGee was a rare individual. He possessed a sense of humor so bizarre that I fully suspect he was kicked out of every class he was in, and suspended from every school he attended. You see, he *farted*. At will, indiscriminately, with vigor, and sometimes shyly—every conceivable way a person can fart. The gross part of me was amused, while the developing ethereal part was embarrassed. But no one else even seemed to notice. They took his idiosyncrasy as naturally as breathing. This, in itself, surprised me.

Mike's predilection allowed me to study the Man—if he was a Man. Was he deliberately trying to cover up his Leprechaun identity? Do self-respecting Imps, playful as they are, pass gas in mixed company uninhibitedly? Or was he such a super-dense Human that he was incapable of ever becoming refined enough to become a Leprechaun? And if so, why did Larry allow him to stay? Mike puzzled me, yet I definitely found him fascinating enough to include in my Journal:

Mike McGee seems to fart like most of us breathe—he doesn't think about it. He doesn't even appear to be aware he's doing it. Perhaps it's for this reason that others accept him. If Mike was trying to get attention, people would call him on it.

Is he so well developed that bodily functions are beneath him—or is he such a good actor that he has everyone fooled? Either way, and as odd as it might seem, I feel the Man (?) can be trusted. Anyone so natural has to be attuned to something higher.

Sally McGee, Mike's Committed, could easily be classified as a Saint. Who else could put up with such an eccentric husband—and on the level of sweetness, Sally can't be surpassed. It's almost as if the more Mike carries on, the more loving and gentle she becomes. I have my doubts about Mike making it to the *Promised Land*, but not Sally—she's a *shoo-in* if ever there was one.

Sean and Sarah Lowrey, on the other hand, are cut from an entirely different bolt of tartan. The best word to describe them is *bland*—as in dull. It's not that they don't have any charm, love of life, or blissful moments. It's more that they seem to blend into the wallpaper. But then, I've heard that the inconspicuous make the best undercover agents because nobody notices them. So who knows?

In spite of their dullness, the Lowreys seem to radiate a quiet urgency—as if this is their last chance to do something special. Who knows, maybe they'll be the first to graduate. But for all I know, Sean and Sarah might be the only *bona fide* Wee Folk of the lot, and are putting on such good acts that no one will ever detect them. They certainly have mastered the art of being inconspicuous.

As for us, I *think* we come off as loving Committeds. After all, this entire adventure began while we were still on our honeymoon. And because of that, we could be seen as dyed-in-the-wool Leprechauns who find love in everything we do. On the other hand, we could also be seen as the most gross, dense Humans, trying our best to *act* like Leprechauns. I don't know how others see us, except that once in awhile, naïve young lads and lasses approach us asking advice. But, as strange as it may seem, I've also noticed sneering on more than one occasion when we showed affection in public.

I'm very happy that Barbara encouraged me to keep the Journal, and to continue writing. It's helped me to sort everything out, and has also been good therapy.

We spent our days and nights minding the Shop, and playing host and hostess to the endless stream of visitors. When the McGees or Lowreys stayed home, we moved between our Shops and theirs.

CHAPTER 16

▼

While the Whereever experience had been quite pleasant, the idea of becoming a Leprechaun seemed as foreign as becoming a *toad*. Before Larry *popped* into my life, I thought we were born one thing, and stayed that way. After all, what Prince in his right mind would ever think of becoming a *toad*? Yet the Leprechauns—or someone—had put the idea in Larry's mind for Man and Imp to switch roles. It had worked from Leprechaun to Man—I myself watched Larry appear and disappear and walk through my desk … and yet his handshake was also very real.

Everyone at Whereever was betting it would work the other way around—that is, for them to transform themselves into Leprechauns. But for me to be absolutely convinced myself, I would really have to move through the desk *on my own and without Larry's assistance.*

Whether the developed Human was the seed for the Leprechaun, or the Leprechaun came first and then raised himself into flesh and bone—I never figured out which came first.… Of course, another possibility is that the two are actually the same, and it's just a matter of where we put our attention—like passing through solid objects versus vanishing. It seems to be a possibility, anyway....

When we found out that Barbara had mistaken sweet Midge for an Angel, my curiosity was aroused—*'is the Angel-Human relationship the same as Leprechaun-Man?'* The idea had been on my mind so much that it eventually ended up in my Journal.

> I've heard that Angels are a transitional state—*one rung on the evolutionary ladder.* A soul rises from the very bottom—where we're cavemen in body and mind—to highly developed, spiritual beings. Now, if Barbara, who must be highly developed, could mistake a Leprechaun or Human for an Angel—or vice versa—then maybe ... just maybe, we're all essentially the same but at different levels....
>
> If this is case, the question becomes, *'Why change from one form to another?'* You know, why not just be who we are and—if we want some variety, think 'Angel' or think 'Leprechaun' ... or whatever form we want to be. What if this whole *Whereever* apprentice thing is just a *game* Larry and his fellow Recruiters have drummed up to make their lives more interesting?
>
> This also suggests to me that the Leprechauns might be trying to fool us. Why don't we take charge, and have them dance to our tune?

I usually use my Journal to state what has happened, but sometimes alternatives and possibilities are included as variations of reality. After all, introspection can be mistaken for being *off your rocker*—mental instability. And if the Leprechauns peg me as a nut case, my stay at Whereever might not be very long. Anyway, while jotting down thoughts, I added this:

> From watching Mike McGee—rather, from listening to him—he doesn't seem to care who's standing right in front of him. Maybe it says more about the *people who ignore him,* than Mike himself—I don't know. Barbara takes everything in stride—her replies are often, 'Don't fret, it'll probably all come out in the wash.'
>
> Maybe she's way up the ladder and I'm on rung number one? If so, that would explain why Larry let Barbara come in the first place—to help me. On the other hand, it could be that I'm up there, and Barbara needs a hand.... Seems unlikely, but it does suggest that two people might be able to climb faster than one, since they can lend each other a helping hand.
>
> Speaking of couples, Larry claims that Leprechauns hold *Committedness* as the highest priority next to being eternally happy and *twinkling*.

I was going to add more to the Larry Log, but Barbara entered the room and said, "Johnny, Sean and Sarah Lowrey have disappeared. Oh, not the way Larry does, or a Gathering—they're just *no longer here.* What's going on?"

"Only one person to ask," I replied, as Larry suddenly appeared.

"Hey, Larry, help us out, will you? Tell us what's going on—did Sean and Sarah pass the test and become permanent Leprechauns, or did they fail and go back to Human life?

They were such good people and, well … we also want to know if whatever happened to them can happen to us—aren't we all in the same boat?"

"Slow down, Mac," soothed the Recruiter. "You're getting all damp about the brow. Everything's happening just as it should. You'll find that it doesn't really matter what happened to them or where they went. You're all that really matters— that is, ya' and yer Barb, and the dandy thing ya' have going here. I suggest that ya' forget who comes and goes, and enjoy yer happiness while ya' have it."

His words obviously didn't answer my questions, but they did act as a progress report. *'Ye' and yer Committed have such a dandy thing going'*—that sounded good. But not hearing a direct answer to my questions was annoying and made me feel suspicious. The fact that the Lowreys could disappear instantly made me wonder, *'Why not us?'*—and I didn't like that one bit.

"Mac, m'lad," said Larry, "you're not satisfied here in Whereever?"

"It's not that, Lare. I'm just curious—no different from you. I mean, it's important to know what all the small print means before signing a contract. Now, did Sean and Sarah go back to their homes in the Human world? Did they go to some other Whereever? And do Humans have a say in where they might be transferred?"

"What questions, Mac. Makes me wonder about yer progress."

"I don't know what you mean…. It's just that I'm curious and want to know what's going on."

"Well lad, as a real estate agent, ya' do like to see the house before ya' buy. So, it seems only fitting that ya' should have yer curiosity satisfied. Who knows, maybe you're ready for the next step—so, tell ya' what, let's take the *Grand Tour*. Aye, and while ya' enjoy yerself, it'll give me a chance to do something I've had on my mind for some time. Brace yerself."

It all happened so fast—like the Lowreys disappearing. So fast that Larry didn't give me any room to ask the questions sprouting in my mind: *'How long will I be gone? Why isn't Barbara coming?'* and *'Where does all of this lead?'*

The quickness of his decision also raised a question that had been on my mind—I feared that I didn't have what it takes to become a Leprechaun. Was Larry taking me on this Tour to see if I could cut it, or was this his way of getting rid of me? Could I be in the same boat as the Lowreys—and, would I find myself back in my real estate office two seconds from now?

All I could do was accept his statement that everything happens as it's supposed to, and follow Larry's lead.

CHAPTER 17

So many events happened in rapid succession that there was no way I could have remembered a thing without the Larry Log—which seemed to irk Larry immensely. It was looking more and more as if the ideal candidates for Leprechaunness would be the ones who *forget* everything Human—those who might not even care who or what was left behind.

Maybe I wasn't an ideal candidate after all?

Larry certainly was one for keeping secrets. Why did he take me on this Tour, something he obviously hadn't planned earlier? Anyway, the *Grand Tour* was so interesting that I wrote down every possible detail, including Austrian shorts and the latest *twinkleness*. Not everything was a surprise, since I'd heard names of the Recruiters from their earlier conference.

Bascomb and Vienna

What a grand place, Vienna! No wonder so many great musicians have lived here. The atmosphere is like a constant song. Lightness and liveliness everywhere, although that may have been because of the mood Larry was in. I felt like waltzing with every step.

Larry took me from one Shop to the next, so I could appreciate the full flavor of this particular Whereever. One Shop *felt like* 'Opera', another *felt like* 'Conductor', and a third *felt like* 'Composer'. Others felt like the different sections of an orchestra. The entire Leprechaun community was like that. It was so completely musical that upon entering the Singers' Shop, I broke spontaneously into song. What brought this on? I'm no singer—why, I can't even carry a tune at all. *Ah, it must be Vienna!*

Bascomb is quite a fellow. While Larry always wears tweeds with that delightful tam-o'-shanter, the European Recruiter actually dons rather stylish Austrian shorts. Oh, why couldn't I have grabbed my camera before Larry whisked me off?

This Recruiter is also as merry as a song. He dances with everyone he meets, and keeps time like a metronome. When I met him, we both laughed and there was instantly a Gathering! My ego told me it was my doing, though there was the sound of a fingersnap in the background ... the same kind we heard in Larry's Whereever. With heavenly voices, harps, and other musical instruments, this Gathering made the others seem like quiet laughter. Thank you, Bascomb Leprechaun!

Lung Chu and Nepal

I didn't have to join the Navy to see the world, after all! From Vienna to Nepal—Austria has music, and Nepal has mountainous silence. It's also cold and windy here. And what a difference between the musical sounds of Vienna and the silence of Nepal! It's as quiet and meditative here as Vienna is musical and active.

The Shops, however, are pretty much the same. Leprechauns everywhere must have used a universal mold. Only slight variations exist, and those come from the proprietors—some have flags and others prayer wheels. But every Shop is actually almost empty. Their purpose seems less social than in North America, and certainly not as musical as Vienna. It's as if their whole purpose is silently performing *whatever,* in Whereever—quite the opposite of the two Whereevers I'd already seen.

Lung Chu reminded me of a Guru or Zen Master. He definitely has the Leprechaun *twinkle,* though he uses it to put others at ease rather than to enliven them. It took me awhile to understand that paradox. Bascomb has the liveliest eyes, but they are deeply calming. I don't know how many eons the fellow has meditated, but he certainly radiated a peaceful silence.

Perhaps it's my aggressive real estate nature, but I feel rather out of place in Nepal. Lung Chu didn't seem to notice me—but then, he didn't pay much attention to anyone. And since I'm just a passer-through, that's probably to be expected. When all is said and done, I'm really tickled that Larry took me along, and that Lung Chu tolerated me.

Pauul and the Congo

It never occurred to me that there could ever be a *black* Leprechaun—but why not? From what I've seen in my Tours, Leprechaunness appears to be a *quality of the soul.* Not based on one's genetics or environment. Pauul and every apprentice is as black as—well, an *African.*

Pauul and his charges showed me that the residents reflect the character of the Recruiter in charge. No great revelation. The pattern became obvious after seeing lively Larry and most of the people in the North American

Whereever, the song-and-dance of Bascomb and the musical Viennese, the silent Lung Chu and the meditative Nepalese.... And now, everything *Congo Africanse*.

Unexpectedly, I was struck by quite a notable difference between *black Africans* and *black Americans*. The natives in the Congo are quite pure, and are much more in touch with the earth and *themselves*. In contrast, many blacks in the 'States seem more like *reactions to the whites*.

The Congo contingent seemed mellow, but not meditatively quiet like the apprentices in Nepal. You know— just totally at ease, since Pauul makes everyone feel relaxed.

Julio in Uberlandia, South America

Hustle—hustle—hustle. That's the feeling in Uberlandia, compared to the meditative Leprechauns of Nepal, and the easy-going African brothers of the Congo. On the one hand, Julio and his apprentices are as calm as church-mice—but on the other hand, they can be as *hyper* as anyone from Chicago or New York. Is this because Julio and his group are a mixture of Native Indian and European Anglo? I don't know, but they're *up one minute and down the next*—like yo-yos.

Julio has arranged the Shops here differently from other Whereevers. One Shop is animated and hyperactive, while the next might be calm and serene. Interesting how even the outward structure of the South American Whereever reflects the bipolarity of Julio and his group. Uberlandia does have its charm, though. After all, they *are* Leprechauns and Leprechaun apprentices—*twinkling* eyes and all.

Julio himself is a master of balancing disparate parts, a job that he does well.

Sidge at the North Pole

This Whereever is full of surprises. For one thing, the number of Native Inuits amazes me—where did they all come from? I asked Sidge, Larry's North Pole counterpart. He laughed, and jokingly replied, "Where have you been?" I didn't know exactly what that meant, but sensed he was telling me that not all Eskimos live in igloos and hunt seals—nowadays, most dwell in villages and enjoy modern technologies.

The apprentices here are probably the most carefree and simplistic beings on earth. I suspect that if the areas of the earth were divided according to the degrees of closeness to Full Leprechaunness, Sidge and the North Pole souls would rate rather high.

Everyone here in the community appears to *resemble* Sidge. Larry says that they are actually *just like him*. No students or apprentices—all Developed Beings. It's actually a bit scary. The other Whereevers have what appears to be a Master Leprechaun with a multitude of followers. Everyone here seems to be equally developed—with no master to follow. Maybe that's due to Sidge's unique ability.

Ooma and the South Pole

If the North Pole surprised me, Ooma's community at the South Pole flabbergasted me. After all, no one lives there—*do they?* I've never heard that the South Pole was inhabited by indigenous people. Of course, scientists and explorers have come, but they're not permanent residents. Yet, here we met swarms of residents as real as the ice under my feet!

Although I haven't seen every Leprechaun and Leprechaun apprentice on earth, my guess is that Ooma's group is comprised of the most unusual selection of Elementals. Check this out, Journal: When Humans overran the Elementals and sent them into hiding, they sought out the most secluded spots on earth. Where's more secluded than the South Pole *where no Human lives?* In other words, the Imps that live here *demand* privacy, and no one argues with them.

In a bit of morbid curiosity, I wonder if any South Pole Leprechauns ever met a half-frozen and starved explorer and asked themselves, *'Where do I go now to keep away from Humans?'* I get the feeling that the South Pole has the highest concentration of long-term unmolested Leprechauns. Here, the shyest of the shy live—souls who absolutely refuse to live anywhere near even the most remote *possibility* of invasion. Eons of isolation seems to have made them indescribably pure. They are the sky, they are the snow, they are the wind, the cold … and the ice. It's almost as if they don't exist at all as physical entities.

All this makes Ooma's job unique. Everywhere else, except possibly at the North Pole, the Recruiter is a *force*. But here, Ooma floats around observing. His job appears to be nothing more than to remain innocuous, though his presence is still noticeable. And while the group might have seen a brave explorer or foolhardy scientist, undoubtedly not one of those intruders ever saw a single Leprechaun! The presence of the Leprechauns here can be explained from their history, yet where did all the apprentices come from?

It also occurs to me that these are the strongest Leprechauns on earth—strong because of their innocence. It really wouldn't surprise me if I were to hear that a South Pole Imp hadn't even winced when most violently threatened by a Human. Down here, they're as innocent as mice that have never seen a cat. May this purity—and that of the entire Antarctic—last forever!

Brian in the Outback

How in the world did this black, curly-haired, Elemental Aborigine with a *nose bone* get the name of *Brian?* I must ask Larry. And, do Aborigines even wear bones? I thought that ornamentation came from Borneo or South America—but not Australia. Anyway, looking at Brian and his crew, it became abundantly clear that I don't know a thing about this *Down Under culture*. Not that Brian is typical—but there are many in this community that resemble him.

It seems that each of these communities draws people from a fairly wide area. The Vienna group is not made of only Viennese—some are from Scandinavia, the Southern Mediterranean, and Scotland. In Brian's Whereever, I see Japanese, Malaysians, Philippinos, Aborigines, and a fair number of English.

The best way to describe Brian is that he's *'not a Brian'*. As far as I can tell, he's one hundred percent Aborigine. This makes him all the more remarkable, since everyone calls him the King—that is, the King of all the Recruiters and maybe all Leprechauns. I wanted to ask Larry, but couldn't find him. Anyway, the extraordinary *twinkle* in his eyes, the look suggesting that he could pull a trick on you while pretending to be serious, and his ineffable lightness, are marks of a true Leprechaun.

He possesses yet another quality the other Recruiters lack. A definite honesty that instills a confident feeling that while he *might* trick you, the chances are he won't. That's what's so unique about him—everyone *trusts* Brian. And because trust is so important among the Wee

Folk—most apparent in their Eternal Commitments to their spouses—this trait serves him very well.

Brian was both an inspiring leader and a great motivator. Rumor has it that his apprentices have surpassed all others in their ability to successfully disappear and re-appear at will—like Midge, but better. The folks under Brian's tutelage certainly mirror this extraordinary Leprechaun. They have the air about them that says, 'I am Royal. I'll succeed. I *will* be a Leprechaun.'

As I wandered around, there was yet another surprise awaiting me—*no Shops in the Outback*. Well, *whatever* in this Whereever! Everyone here lives just like their Aboriginal leader—free and uninhibited.

Brian *looks* like a pure Aborigine with his features, dark skin, curly hair, and that awesome nose bone. *National Geographic* should film this guy. He even grunts—luckily, not the way Mike McGee does. Anyway, if I were identifying pure Leprechauns and pure Humans in a line-up, it would be hard to pick out Brian as a Leprechaun—unless I saw the *twinkling eyes*, that is. Well … and that he appears so light on his feet that he could probably walk on rainbows.

I really do think we'll meet again. Hmmm—it makes me wonder if the whole purpose of the *Grand Tour* was all about meeting Brian! Larry is fine as a mentor, but he has a tinge of unreliability—compared to Brian, anyway.

Brian is completely and dependably … *himself.*

Conclusions and Questions

The Tour was an amazing success.

Not all Leprechauns are the same. I enjoyed them all, but would have enjoyed meeting even more.

Some I liked, some I really liked, and others I would almost trust my life with.

Can apprentices like me visit other Whereevers by will, or do we need a Recruiter to guide us?

Why did Larry take me on the Tour anyway?

Why didn't Barbara come along?

Good night, Journal.

CHAPTER 18

▼

The *Grand Tour* was a most remarkable experience, but it was good to be back with Barbara, enjoying the Shops and Village—and the whole North American scene. And after visiting all of the Whereevers, I concluded that Larry's was the one that felt most like *home*.

Things were, however, a bit different now. Barbara had become a minor celebrity, and our Shop was one of the most popular in the Village. My dear wife seemed to have transformed into *Mrs Congeniality*, being as full of gaiety as much as any Leprechaun.

In my absence, Sean and Sarah Lowrey had been replaced by Ted and Susan Margoles—an affable couple who added charm to the place. The two were almost the opposite of the somber Lowreys. Mike McGee continued his peculiar habit, while Sally was just as sweet as ever. But I was most impressed by the changes in Barbara.

"You seem to glow, dear. You've gained a certain relaxation that really becomes you. That *barb-like* quality Larry joked about seems to have dissolved. In its place is a wonderfully magnetic quality. The Tour was apparently quite good for both of us."

Her euphoric beam nearly blinded me, so I didn't press for details. Curiously, her development seemed to be exponential—something really big must have happened while I was away. The difference between her pre-Tour 'catching people' and her present 'mesmerizing people' was more subtle and quite remarkable.

We entertained hundreds in our Kindergarten and Real Estate Shops—it was really a lot of fun. Had I sold houses to one percent of the visitors, we would have been set for life. In keeping with the Whereever tradition, Barb and I left the McGees and Margoleses, and visited elsewhere in the afternoons. Arm in arm, we bounced from Clothing Shop to Blacksmith Shop to Candy Shop. And everywhere we visited, Barbara was greeted warmly and treated like someone special.

"Larry," I said, when we met our host in the General Shop. "This learning by observation that you talk about, sometimes it just takes too long. Can't you simply spell out what's happened to Barbara—and what she is being groomed for?"

"*Groomed for,* Mac?" answered the Wee One innocently. "Is *grooming* something ya' picked up on the Tour?"

"It is," I said flatly. "The entire Experiment is aimed at grooming. Training, development, *grooming*—there're all the same, aren't they? Anyway, you seem to have singled out Barbara for something special. As her husband, I'd like to know what that is. And while you're at it...."

The Recruiter looked up. His eyes *twinkled* as if to distract me. Something was happening, but it was just below the surface. Whatever it was, I wanted to know.

"Well, Mac," Larry said finally, "'tis worth pondering. But, like everything else, only time will tell."

'Something big is afoot,' struck my mind like lightning. *'Is Barbara close to reaching the state where she can pass as a Leprechaun? Have I been farmed off so I'll be out of the way? Or, am I being groomed for something else? Why aren't Barbara and I developing hand-in-hand, rather than what appears to be different speeds—and directions?'*

It was obvious that Larry was reading my mind, and that he'd decided not to answer me. My conclusion was that I would have to find my own answers—and that would take time.

One day, an extraordinary event occurred while eccentric Mike McGee was talking to a group of teenagers at their Hangout Shop. Naturally, the guy let loose with one of his characteristically gaseous backfires—and the teenagers, all new residents, took it as a challenge. Being teenagers, they began their own performances, every one trying to outdo Mike. It took only seconds for the entire Shop to explode in merriment, and a joy so grand that it became contagious.

The entire Village transformed into a Gathering.

Gatherings, when not stimulated by Larry or one of the Recruiters, are uncommon and usually generated by older souls. For this young group to create such a Grand Happening seemed a bit unusual. That is, unless Mike had actually been the sole cause—providing further evidence that he might be more than meets the *ear*.

The very next day, Larry talked to me in a tone less jovial than usual.

CHAPTER 19

▼

My talk with Larry was so unbelievable that I have to rely on my Journal to recall everything that happened between us:

I can't believe that Larry lectured me about the *importance* of the Experiment. And it was pretty heavy, coming from a Race known for its lightness. The gist of it seemed to be that I was *not* developing at all well. Not even close to achieving full Leprechaunness, as others were.

After being questioned, Larry said I think too much. Apparently I haven't let go of my Humanness yet, like during my first visit here. Larry said something like, 'You're too much *in yer head*—analyzing, reasoning, doubting, thinking. Leprechauns *feel*, Mac. Why things feel right or happy or gay *doesn't matter*.' Well, it is true that I get joy from figuring things out and understanding them. That's all well and good in my world, but not in Leprechaun lands.

Oh, Larry also told me that Barbara was developing well, *unlike me*. Now that was really too much—considering that Leprechauns *supposedly don't judge or compare!* In total frustration, I simply lost it, and slugged him squarely on the jaw. In that single act, I had committed the Leprechaun *sin of sins*. Since violence is what drove them underground before, this act might mean they never show themselves again.

Of course, that was the end of my apprenticeship for Leprechaunhood. Hitting Larry demonstrated that I was an obvious brute, and a violent one at that. It wasn't at all necessary to tell Larry that the whole Experiment was off—that's what he had been trying to tell me before I belted him. Not having anything more to lose, my angry words spewed at Larry's now-invisible figure. *'Fine, Larry, so Barbara and I'll pack our bags and leave. And by the way, don't be surprised if this Whereever and every other Leprechaun Community is blown to smithereens.'*

It was a good thing that Larry had become stronger than when we first met, because my words struck him angrily like daggers, hand grenades, and bombs. Somehow, he must have been expecting this, because he remained relatively unscathed. Larry countered by telling me that while I was on the Grand Tour, Barbara had done two things. She had passed the Leprechaun test—so she could remain in Whereever forever if she chose. And then he grumbled and mumbled something else that I couldn't understand.

My fiery reply was that Larry was a *filthy liar—and a wimpy hypocrite*. I could no longer believe his song and dance about Commitment being a great virtue, because Larry was telling me that he was essentially breaking up a couple. Demanding that he lead me to my wife *that instant,* I threateningly insisted that we'd settle what choice she's made *in front of me,* adding for emphasis, 'if you don't, Larry, you and your midgets will have a *real* reason to hide!'

My doom was certainly sealed with that one, yet Larry again threw me a curve ball. With unexpected calmness, he informed me that he has never lied in his endless life. And he even had the nerve to add that, 'married on earth' is not the same as, 'Committed amongst Leprechauns'. Apparently, you have to be married *in Whereever* for the bond to be held *sacred* by Leprechauns!

'*Oh, so Mr Super Recruiter Leprechaun is making the rules as he goes, is he?*' I accused him, my temper rising. To no avail, I again demanded to know where my wife was. And then, just wanting to get my hands on him, I yelled, '*Tell me where you are, you dirty rascal! Are you Leprechaun enough to show yourself?*'

That tricky Leprechaun must've figured that he had the upper hand as he hovered invisibly out of my sight—and reach. His jibberish actually continued with things like, 'what the lass does is up to her,' and, 'I cannot dictate what a free soul does, nor would I care to.'

Unable to believe my ears, I even threatened the extinction of his race … but to no avail. That's all it took—right, Journal? Except for one big thing—there was this problem of how to return to my real estate office in the Human world. The only known way to accomplish this would be for Larry to hold my hand. But I was more than sure that the instant that happened, he'd find a way to be rid of me forever.

Oh that charlatan—he must've expected me to be foolish or blind enough to fall into the trap of holding his faerie hands again, just to escape and be free of him. A feeling of '*good riddance Leprechaun Whereevers*' washed over my weary mind, giving way to the realization that I might *never* see Barbara again.

So here I am, a Man without a country—not on earth and not in Leprechaundom. Once an eager and promising apprentice ... I was now nothing more than an unwelcome Man booted into the *twilight zone* of Whereever. Can't talk to the folks in the Shops, can't see my wife ... can't go up, down, or sideways—I was fit to be tied, but no one dared to come close enough to try.

It finally occurred to me that ranting in my Journal would get me nowhere. I took a deep breath, put the pen aside, and tried to get my bearings.

'Why hasn't Barb talked to me and explained her decision? Are they holding her somewhere against her will? Have they brainwashed her so well—while I was on the Tour—that she became one of them? Whatever happened isn't fair, nor is it right. Barbara and I should have had a chance to resolve this ourselves.'

Before departing, my mind quieted somewhat and finally I concluded, *'Que sera, sera'*—whatever will be, will be. If Barbara was so far gone that she didn't know what was going on, what could I do at this instant? Not knowing where she was, there would be too much of a ruckus if I tried to find her and take her with me. We really needed to talk, but it was time for me to leave Whereever *now*.

Perhaps if everything could be sorted out, we would find a way to get together again. Meanwhile, my thoughts roamed as I roamed about the land. Oh, it seemed like I must've walked a thousand miles—as if I'd been inspecting houses on foot. The change and exercise and was good for me, and it helped clear the cobwebs out of my head.

Late in the day, I met a most unusual individual. He was what the Leprechauns call a *Grumpy*.

CHAPTER 20

▼

"Aha," said the stranger, shaking my hand with gusto, "another outcast."

"It seems so."

"I'm Glenn Mye rhymes-with-eye—and let me guess who you are. Off the top of my head, I'd say you're Johnny McMann, the real estate Man married to Barbara. And the only one bold enough to wallop a Leprechaun since I've been a resident of the *never-never-land* of Whereever."

"That was a mouthful. Tell me how you know so much about me?"

"Connections on the inside, of course. And by the way, you're not the only one who's been booted out of Whereever—out on his own."

"You lived in Whereever, then?"

"Until I figured out what was really going on. By the way, everyone's surprised Larry let you keep your Journal so long. Or keep it at all, for that matter. The Leprechauns don't even like the *possibility* that their ways might become public knowledge. I kept telling the others it was just a matter of time until you left or were tossed out."

Glenn was a good Man. He was real—in fact, the most real being I'd seen in some time. My defenses eased up when he said he was a Grumpy. "So there are others?"

"Yes. There are three of us. But listen, the longer we stay outside, the easier it'll be for the *Leps* to find us on their radar."

"*Leps? Radar?*"

"Leps … Leprechauns, and you know—intuition, ESP, or whatever you want to call it. As long as we hide in the cave, we're okay."

"Sounds ominous. Still, I'm really happy to have some company—it's pretty desolate out here."

As Glenn scooted me toward the cave, he said, "I have to hand it to you, Johnny. Not many people stand up to Larry and punch him in the snoot. They figure they'll be turned into toads or something, if they do."

"Frankly Glenn, there was no thinking to it. He irked me so much that I would've hit him even if he'd been a tiger with his mouth wide open."

"So I gathered from my own intuition and a friend who spies for the Leprechauns."

"Oh, spies and intuition? I thought we'd left all that behind."

"Hey, it works. And the funny thing is that the Leps *do not have a monopoly on mental powers*. I can read their minds faster than they can vanish."

"Then why didn't you become a Leprechaun? Or are you one who's just testing me?"

"I wouldn't be a Leprechaun if it was the last thing on earth," Glenn said boldly. "It's hard enough being Human. But they did have me going with their promises. Trouble is, I was too much for them. You know, because of figuring out their plans and all."

"And just what is this plan? I've sensed that something was going on, though I never quite nailed it down. One thing that's for sure is there are an awful lot of unanswered questions—and too much secrecy."

"What better way to take over the world?"

"*What?*"

"That's right—the longer they remain secret, the stronger they become. So, in time they might just be able to take over. In the meantime, they keep doing it to us."

"*Doing it?* Would you mind clarifying that, so I don't have to read between the lines and misinterpret?"

By this time, we were in the cave, an underground cavern that looked solid enough to withstand a bombing. "Best place in the whole area," said Glenn. "It's so dense that no matter how psychic the Leps are, they can't penetrate the granite. We're safe in here."

"Great. I'm tired of all their nonsense. Larry knows my every thought—and what he doesn't pick out of my brain, he gets from what is written in my Journal."

"There you have it," said Glenn. "But here, we have our privacy."

The cave felt homey to me—and was pretty much the opposite of the ethereal, gossamer, translucent world of the Elementals. Maybe it was my affinity for land that came through. "So, Mye-that-rhymes-with-eye, tell me the straight scoop, will you?"

"Okay. Leps brainwash the apprentice Humans. Didn't they tell you to surrender everything including your mind, body, *and* soul? The closer you are to one hundred percent Leprechaun, the more completely they have you. That is, they have your very *being*. And once they have that, they are able to do what they want with you."

"But we're still ninety-nine point nine-nine-nine percent or less—not one hundred, aren't we?"

"Right—and that's our only hope. Slim, but that last percentage point is what keeps us Human, and able to function on our own. When all's said and done, you know, we can't become Leprechauns any more than they can become Humans," concluded Glenn. "But as long as we think we can become Leprechauns, and surrender to their will, they can *manipulate* us and control our lives completely."

"Sounds like the ultimate conspiracy."

"Bingo!"

Although the cave really was very earthy—solid rock, dirt, gravel, dampness, and darkness—it was also relatively cozy. Humans had obviously lived there for some time. Not that it had wall-to-wall carpeting or crystal chandeliers, but it *felt* inhabited. I was comfortable with the other People here, and this cave dwelling.

"Well, Glenn, nice to know that I still have a mind of my own. From what you say, that's what's going to keep me from becoming *one of them*. And you—you seem to have your wits about you. How long have you and the others been here? I've never even heard about you guys."

"No one in Faerie Land will ever tell you about us, either. If anyone knew about us, they might begin to wonder. And once that happens, the Leps' control diminishes—they can't afford that. By the way, it's a good sign that you're here. It shows that the Leps aren't too close to taking over."

"That and Mike McGee's farts?" I chuckled.

Glenn Mye rhymes-with-eye laughed as he hadn't since becoming a Grumpy. "Bravo Johnny, you picked the needle out of the haystack—yes, Mike's one of us! And, you know what? He is so good that he has them fooled. The fact that you pegged him says a lot about you. *Ha!* They think they've converted Mike one hundred percent, but the truth is that as long as he keeps blowing good ones, he's holding onto himself!"

"Actually, I wasn't sure whether he was a Leprechaun or one of us."

"No matter. It's alright, as long as they think he's one of them. That's the fun of it all—he's the only one who passed their test by faking it."

"I didn't think you could fake this kind of thing. You're either one hundred percent Leprechaun, or you're Human—dense as they would say."

"Hey, people fake polygraphs all the time. Well, Mike's so good that he's fooled the most intuitive of the lot—Brian. To the point that the nose-boned King even chose him to be a mole."

"Mole?"

"You know, the undercover agent who spies and gives away secrets. Brian has entrusted Mike to pass on information about the apprentices."

"Mike McGee, a double agent—and to think that his farts never gave him away." But I didn't put this comment in my Journal. I figured that if I did, and Larry or Brian ever got a hold of it, then everyone including Mike would be in trouble. It seemed that both sides were being secretive.

"Yeah, a double agent. Unfortunately, Mike has to let a few worthy souls slip through the cracks in order to maintain his cover. He can't lie about everyone, but yes, Barbara is still one of us."

"She is? Oh, I was so worried that she might be a goner." No news could have been more welcome at the moment, especially since I didn't know where I was, where to go, what to do, or how to do it.

"Glenn, you're a life-saver."

CHAPTER 21

"Just remember, Johnny, leave the cave only if you have some dense object like a branch, log, or maybe a rock—they're physical enough to throw the Leps' radar off. Otherwise the little buggers will detect you for sure." No sooner than he said that, than two men dashed into the hollow.

"I was just telling Johnny never to leave the cave without a dense cover," said Glenn, "and here you are as if you were going to your offices on *Wall Street*. Come on, boys, be serious!"

"Hey Johnny, I'm glad you found us. Mike passed the word that you're okay. My name's Stan Lew."

"And I'm Ben Bow. You seem surprised?"

"Only that I don't remember seeing you guys at Whereever. Glenn says...."

"That's because we've all been here for awhile. Didn't Glenn fill you in?"

"Not many details. Not even how long you've all been on your own."

"Forget them for the moment," warned Glenn. "Boys, you must attend to your camouflage. Once the Imps find out where we are, it's all over. They'll *know* we're plotting against them."

"What difference does that make?" I asked innocently.

"Every difference—because the first thing a Leprechaun does when he feels threatened, is vanish. And once they're gone, we won't have a chance. So, *cover up when you leave!*"

"Anyway," said Stan, "Mike says you slugged Larry like he's never been hit before—wish I'd been there. *Darn,* I should have been the one doing the slugging!"

The conversation continued while the three gathered sticks and built a fire.

"I'm starved," said Glenn. "What did you guys find that's edible—anything?"

Only then did it occur to me that I hadn't eaten in a very long time. "How do they do that? Keep you from eating? They absorb food by looking at it, but we need to eat the real thing."

"It's all in the ninety-nine point nine-nine-nine percent, Johnny. They become so refined that when they do their *whatever,* there's not even a desire for nourishment." Glenn blew on the fire, and the smoke slowly filled the cave. Stan and Ben stood at the entrance and waved the smoke out.

"Their *whatever,* by the way," explained Glenn, "means *power of suggestion*. When you're that refined, all a Lep has to do is say 'be like us,' and we are. Of course, *being like them* and *being them* are two different things. We Grumpys know that—unfortunately the other apprentices don't, and remain in a hypnotic daze." The four of us devoured the two rabbits Stan and Ben had snared. Afterward, we lay down and rested—it had been a long time since I'd slept.

The men knew they were in for a barrage of questions. Not only was I a newcomer, but the guys apparently knew me to be a real question-asker—so they put off the inevitable as long as possible. The first question was, "How can we break up this conspiracy?"

The three laughed. "Maybe you should concentrate on how to stay warm tonight, and what we're going to have for breakfast. Overtaking the *Planet of the Leps* can come later—when we have the strength."

I paid no attention. "The way I see it, there are several possibilities. One, we free the poor apprentices who don't really know what's being done to them. You know, like the story of Spartacus, who successfully led a smaller and untrained group of oppressed people in fighting for their freedom against much larger armies of the mighty Roman Empire. Otherwise, we try to weaken the control Larry and the others have over Whereever. Then, tackle them where they're the weakest—where is that, anyway?"

"Very astute," said Glenn, as he searched for more food. "Problem is, they've got the world by the tail."

"How so?"

"Because they've convinced everyone that they're good angel-like beings. You know, laughing, mischievous little buggers who don't really do any harm. Moreover, since they don't physically exist in the first place, no one will take us seriously."

"Not even the apprentices?"

"Especially the apprentices, but for a different reason. You forget, Johnny, they've been brainwashed to think that becoming a Leprechaun is the reason they've been put on earth. They'll be the last ones to join a revolution."

"So it comes down to changing their thinking?"

"Look," said Glenn, his eyes shining because he'd found an edible root that had slipped everyone else's notice, "thinking is good, but since Leps *feel* rather than think, we need another approach. People think Leprechauns are *cool,* and an endangered species—if they exist at all. By the way, those timid little creatures have also seen to it that everyone believes they are not only the good guys, but Man *is evil.* Supposedly, we so bludgeoned the Wee Things that Humans are considered monsters through and through."

Ben watched the last of the root disappear into Glenn's mouth and said, "Man, but I wish I had a banana split!"

"Come on guys, you talk as if you've given up—but I don't intend to. We have this problem, and...."

"Cool your heels, new-boy-in-the-cave. Or you may wind up like Spartacus in his final battle. Anyway, you haven't been listening to what we've been saying. The better the Leprechauns look, the worse we look. And we—the Grumpys—are called the worst of the worst. That means everything we do is seen as *wrong.*"

"Hey guys," I pleaded. "Come down to earth. We *have* to stop them—*they have my wife.*"

The three paused in concern. "Look Johnny, we feel for you. But remember that we've all been here awhile. Mike's doing his best, and we're all doing what we can. But the Leps have public opinion, their mesmerizing magic, and momentum on their side."

"Three cheers for giving up!" I said, and not too pleasantly. "The problem with you guys is that for all you're doing, I haven't heard a single thing that you've actually accomplished—or have in the works. Sending coded messages to a *mole* is great, but it's not leading anywhere. So my suggestion is this—we *change* their thinking and feeling by showing them that they aren't as powerful as they believe. It would drop their self-esteem like a hot rock in water. And when we weaken their hold and get the upper hand, down they go."

"And how do we do that, Mr Problem Solver?" asked Ben, who had obviously thought of this earlier.

"Tackle them where they're most vulnerable, of course. And I have an idea what that is. You see, I took a Tour of all the Whereevers in the world. And, there's one Lep that every other Leprechaun adores and idolizes ... maybe even worships. All we have to do is dethrone him—King Brian."

Everyone looked at me. They were so shocked that they forgot how hungry they were. They thought they'd already heard of every possible way to destroy the Leprechauns' hold. Finally, Stan said, "Why, Johnny McMann, you do go *straight for the jugular!*"

"At least I have your attention—and I'm right, *aren't I?*"

"Yes you are," said Glenn. He looked at Stan and Ben, and said, "You know, between farts, Mike McGee told me that Johnny had taken the Tour and written an account in his Journal."

"Now get a load of that," said Glenn as if he'd sat down to a plate of mashed potatoes and gravy. "Larry was right. Johnny's Journal may indeed be the very downfall of the Leps. Keep talking, Johnny—how do we bring down Brian? Because once we have him, everyone else will fall down like dominoes. He *is* the key."

"Specifically, what's his weakness?" echoed Mike.

"Ego, what else?" As the moment stretched out, Larry's Cheshire-Cat grin must've crept across my face.

My new cave-mates looked at one other and fell mute. They'd been alone so long that it was obvious I would have to do all the thinking and planning for them. "Look guys, everyone in Leprechaundom calls Brian the King. So all we have to do is show them that he's not so high and mighty, *and that he can be tricked by Humans*—who they think are so dense. The poor fellow then loses all credibility."

In a near-silent undertone, someone muttered, *"But how do you trick the King of Tricksters?"*

CHAPTER 22

▼

Lying on my makeshift bed, I realized that a great deal of my happiness came from simply having a place to rest my weary bones and some food in my stomach. Although I had only a few bites of rabbit, it was quite satisfying—yet made me crave more. Getting Barbara back and stopping the conspirators was certainly worth any amount of discomfort. And as rough as my stay at Cave City might be, it was better than the Leprechauns' magical sleep deprivation and starvation routine.

The longer I lay there, the more old familiar Human sensations began returning. Larry and his Clan must have gotten me close to being a full-fledged Leprechaun, because I'd nearly forgotten about my own body. But now—*oh, there's a twitch in my left eye, a pain in a molar; and yet another sensation in my ear!* Unbelievable that ears and teeth can be so sensitive—must be why people take so many pain relievers.

This place certainly makes a good, earthy *decompression chamber.* The others had appointed the cave well, considering they had few tools. It was big enough that it could even provide an ideal hideout for a few pirate gangs or robbers.

Thinking like a realtor, I realized that an enterprising agent could rent each compartment as a back-to-earth condominium, naturally isolated and secure from most outside influences! People could own a rustic cave in the suburbs—and who could boast that these days? A hungry mosquito zinged me and began drawing blood, reminding me that it would be a good idea to install a few screen doors.

Ben and Stan returned empty-handed from their morning hunting trip. Only Glenn had found any eatables, which were two brown things that resembled wrinkled potatoes, and their condition was questionable. When Glenn handed me my two-tablespoon share, I replied, "Why don't we raise a garden instead of scrounging like wild animals?"

"Are you kidding? Then the Leps would know where we are. Besides, where would we find seeds?"

"Come on, Johnny, we've been over this many times. You can't fight shadows—worse, shadows that vanish! Our only hope is your *Master Plan*."

I was happy to get my mind off my stomach. "Well, here's a thought—what if I surrender?"

"Giving up so soon?" asked Stan.

"You don't understand. I *pretend* to surrender—walk around looking distraught, and cower back to Larry with my tail between my legs. Apologize for everything, agree to become the best Human-Leprechaun ever, gain his confidence, *and then....*"

"You've seen too many *James Bond* movies, my friend," interrupted Stan.

"Even though we're dealing with *spirits,* we still have to be realistic," added Ben. "You can do better than that, can't you, Johnny?"

"Maybe it'd work *because* of its simplicity. I could surely pull it off, because it's easy for a lovesick guy to look like he's lost it! Hey, Mike's not the only one who can fake a polygraph test."

"Baloney," said Ben, almost enjoying his brown, wrinkled meal. "The Leprechauns have their antennae out as far as Mars. You'd have to be the world's greatest actor."

"Not if Barbara is there, or I'm thinking about her—then, it would look real."

The three conferred with their eyes.

"I think," said Glenn, the group's spokesman, "we'll leave the undercover work to Mike. No offense, Johnny, but he's been at it for some time now. You'd have to re-program yourself. And from the urgency you're displaying, it appears that you don't want to take the time."

Silence.

"Whatever," I replied absentmindedly.

"But how else can we de-throne Brian and wake up the apprentices?" asked Stan.

"I don't know. But I do know that living like cavemen is ridiculous—we can't just wait. How about this? We go back to earth and create land development projects that will virtually wipe out the Leprechaun strongholds. You know, demolish their sacred hide-outs. We'll make it look as if we're doing good things for Mankind. We actually would be, even though our primary purpose is going to be ridding the world of Leprechauns. In this way, we can save Barbara and all apprentices in the various Whereevers, and do the little buggers in—all at the same time."

"There's one problem—one very big problem," said Glenn. "How to get back to our Human Realm?"

"You've lost it, Johnny—you're trying to strike out blindly on your latest daydreams, in order to bring down their entire Empire. And, here we were thinking you'd be our *Savior*," concluded Ben.

"Then," I said dramatically, "we're left with only one alternative."

Stan flippantly added, "This ought to be good. And what is the only alternative, if I might ask?"

"Rather than attacking them physically, we do it mentally. We beat them at their own game—*remove a thorn with a thorn.*"

"That's what we've been doing all along," said Ben, sad that all that remained of his breakfast was a brown stain on his dirty hand. "And it hasn't worked yet."

"Yes, but you guys have been working from *inside* the cave," I retorted. "And starving, to boot. I say we return to the real world and deliberately undermine the notion that Leprechauns are the sweet little nothings they've conned everyone into believing. Link them with trolls, goblins, and bogey-men. Then tell everyone that if you see a Leprechaun, slam him into the ground—don't be all cutesy with them, chatting and being nice."

"Now, does it still sound like I have *cave-fever?*"

CHAPTER 23

▼

Having just returned to the cave with a hat full of berries and a head full of fresh ideas, I felt a fresh wave of confidence. "All right," I announced, thinking my head had been cleared of wildness, "I've decided what I'm going to do."

"*You've* decided what *you're* going to do?" retorted Glenn authoritatively. "It seems that you haven't been here long enough to realize that the only way to accomplish anything is *by committee*. When one person acts alone, he...."

"*Yes, yes,*" I said impatiently. "We're *all* going to be in on it—in fact, that's the only way my new *brain child* will work."

"Well, since you're going to tell us anyway—let's hear it, then. You did bring us some tasty berries." Everyone munched with wordless gusto. As soon as I'd licked my fingers, I continued, "We simply attack them from all sides simultaneously."

"Bravo!" said Ben, almost choking on his berries, "and who gets the *backside?*"

"I'm serious."

"I'm sure you are," said Glenn. "It's just that, as soon as we attack...."

"*Gentlemen!* As long as we do nothing, they become stronger and we become weaker, so just hear me out. One of us tries to get other apprentices on our side; another works on them, psychically and mentally zapping them; and a third figures out how to capture King Brian. But Leprechauns aren't stupid—they'll know mighty fast that they're under attack, and they no longer rule the roost. And finally, after we have Brian, I'll go back to my real estate office where I know a few politicians and land developers who are just itching to start big-time projects. Can't you see, lads, Larry and his gang will head for cover, and this time for good!"

"*And we thought he'd cleared his head,*" replied Glenn with disappointment.

Everyone sat silently finishing their berries. A stick snapped in the fire and the red sparks flew onto the dirt floor of the cave.

"You're all hesitating because you have no sense of urgency. But I have *every* reason because of my wife. For all I know, they may have changed Barbara so much that she's sprouted wings and can vanish and materialize at will—or is otherwise past the point of no return."

Silence.

Glenn looked up. "That reminds me, Johnny. When you punched Larry, what did you hit—*solid or air*?"

"What difference does it make?"

Glenn explained, "it makes all the difference in the world—you see, there's this little known secret I came across while in Whereever. If you touch air, then the Lep's all *spirit* and therefore beyond reach. But, if you find him to be solid—you know, dense like a Human—then you *can* gain power over him."

"*You're kidding,*" I said excitedly.

"No, dead serious."

"Well, Glenn, you may have just said the magic words, and I don't mean 'dead serious'—rather, 'gaining power over them'! *Don't you see*—we entice Larry to appear, and when he shakes hands—with one of our *dense* hands, of course—we grab him, and it's all over."

"What's over?"

"His reign of terror is over, because now he's in *our* power. On the other hand, I could slug him a real solid punch and send him into next week. But either way, he's ours."

"Brilliant!" said Ben, sarcastically. "And what may I ask, here in the Land of Wherever, are you going to do with a cold-cocked Leprechaun?"

I swooned as melodramatically as possible. "What do we do with him—*ransom* him, that's what!"

"Hmm," hummed Glenn. "That's great for your revenge, Johnny. But the idea was to halt their entire movement, not just resolve your grudge."

"You've been staring at cave walls too long, my friend. Once Larry is in our power, I tell him, '*I will hold on to you forever if you don't call Brian in for a chat.*' He'll probably think two Leprechauns can outwit one Human any day, so he'll agree. And then we take *him* out too. With the two of them captured, we will have bargaining power! Don't you see—if we have the Leprechaun King, the Recruiters will do *anything* to get him back. Then we can demand that they stop this out-rageous Experiment!"

Finally, everyone in the cave smiled.

Glenn nodded his head, then said, "No wonder Larry kicked you out, Johnny. He knew you could be a real threat."

Stan agreed that it was a good idea. "Good thinking, Johnny. But it raises a question about Larry—why did he take you on the Tour, anyway? Leprechauns only do that, I'm told, if there's a possibility the Human is ready to graduate, to move up a rung."

"Maybe he thought it would be better to have the enemy with him on his own side, rather than elsewhere working against him—you know that old saying. What other reason could there be? I sure don't know."

"Me either, Johnny. It's an interesting idea about grabbing Larry and Brian. Unfortunately, I see two big flies in the oint-ment," interjected Mike.

"What's that?"

"First, tricking Larry into becoming dense. He'll be very wary—and especially so if he sees us Grumpys around. And second, drawing King Brian into our trap—you see, while we can monitor what our captured Larry may tell him, we have no control over what is said."

CHAPTER 24

▼

It was a rough night, and not just because of the cold dirt floor. How to nab Larry and Brian churned in my mind constantly. Sure, I could grab a Leprechaun in my imagination, *but in reality?* The problem grew bigger and bigger as I mentally saw my quarries disappear every time action was taken to capture them.

At around five in the morning while putting a log on the fire to keep the cave warm, an idea came to me and I announced, "If we can't get Larry to manifest here, then we simply have to trick him in Whereever!"

Everyone heard me, but no one responded. The boys didn't want to face the damp morning until they had to, and they also didn't want to disillusion me.

"Come on guys, I know you're awake. We're only this far from blowing the conspiracy wide open," I held thumb and forefinger microscopically apart. "Why can't we trick those tricksters?"

"Because Larry's too tricky," moaned Glenn, "and he's been doing it for eons. He knows every trick in the book—in fact, I suspect he wrote it."

"Baloney! Sometimes the greatest con artist is the easiest to con. I tell you...."

"Tell me in the morning, Johnny. After we've had enough sleep to care."

"Glenn, there *has* to be a way to get him solid enough to grab."

"Maybe there is, my friend, but don't you see? The Recruiter only changes his denseness when he's among Humans—to convince them he's a Leprechaun. The bottom line is that he simply doesn't turn solid on his own turf."

"But Glenn, what if he's led to believe he's not on his own turf?"

"Wait until morning, okay?"

I ignored my new friend. *"I have it.* We tidy up the cave and make it look like a real Human dwelling, a place where he could manifest if the circumstances were favorable."

"Hmmm," everyone groaned simultaneously.

"We make a solid front—behave the way *real Humans* do."

"I suppose we could even fart like Mike."

"Why not? Then we tell Larry we're sick and tired of living like a bunch of cavemen. That we either want to return to being Human, or become one hundred percent Leprechaun."

"Keep talking. One ear is listening, though the other is sound asleep."

"Then we put out our hand for a shake—a typical Human gesture. And when he puts forth his hand, we hold on—*forever*."

"Interesting," said Glen, both ears awake now. "And when we have one hand, someone grabs his other—then there's no escape for him. Not to mention the other two sitting on him until he acknowledges defeat."

A moment of silence reigned—only the crackling fire whispered.

Glenn yawned and said, "I suppose it's also possible that once we have Larry, we may not even need to capture King Brian."

"I say we get a little more shut-eye," moaned Stan.

CHAPTER 25

▼

While all the Leprechaun busyness was going on—Experiments, Shops, Tours, Gatherings, Recruiting—life in the Human Realm also progressed. When I didn't show up at my office as scheduled, Sheila became inquisitive.

When Sheila wondered, so did Tammy—Barbara's friend and Maid of Honor. And although Tammy's husband, Tory, usually kept his nose out of his wife's personal concerns, he was pulled into this because Pam fretted. But that wasn't the end of it—Pam Clarke, Barry's wife and recent house-purchaser, had befriended Barbara's friends and also joined the circle of curiosity.

"It's not as if we *need* Johnny right now," said Sheila, "because it's mostly paperwork anyway. But Mr McMann closed such good sales. And while we could coast for awhile, it's good to keep the listings active."

"I know what you mean," said Tory. "Besides, Johnny's a smart fellow. He won't let his business bottom out just for an extended honeymoon, no matter how great it is."

"It's not like Barbara to be out of touch for so long, unless she's sprawled out on a beach in the South Pacific or isolated from all means of communication," remarked Tammy.

"Good point," said Sheila, professionally. "But, I'll make some inquiries anyway. People with whom Mr McMann plays golf, poker—all the guy stuff. The real estate network is fairly good at keeping tabs on its major players."

"And I'll ask around the tea and coffee groups," said Tammy. "Someone may know where Barb is."

Beyond their close friends and business acquaintances, however, no one had the slightest idea how to start a real search. And, with no sign of foul play, they weren't about to call in the police. All the McMann friends could do was wait patiently, expecting Johnny and Barbara to return in their own time.

CHAPTER 26

▼

'As long as people experience bliss, or told that they are, little things seem to go unnoticed—like my absence in Whereever,' I reflected. It also flashed through my mind that Larry couldn't say, 'Did you know that Johnny ran away, and we'll probably never see him alive again?' But, he could imply that I was on another Tour, or some other important Leprechaun business.

Either Barbara was so blissed out in Whereever, or mentally conditioned to the point where she wouldn't even be concerned about my absence. And why?—I had been away on real estate matters for days, and she never used to complain. So, if Larry and his crew were grooming Barbara for some super job, she would have been too preoccupied to notice my absence.

Unbeknownst to me, Larry apparently wanted harmony so much that he constantly distracted Barbara by glorifying the new Shopmates, Ted and Susan Margoles. He never mentioned where the Lowreys might have gone—or me. He just showed up in the Shop unexpectedly, and bamboozled the Margoleses with sweet talk. His constant praise and distracting pranks somehow managed to keep Barbara from suspecting anything.

The only one in the Village not fooled was Mike McGee, which was not surprising, since he was one of the rare ones who never let himself be swayed by all the blissful happiness and joy. So when Mike sensed something was amiss, he contacted the Grumpys in the cave. "Glenn, keep on the lookout for Johnny McMann. He's outcast material if I ever saw it—questions everything and puts Larry on the spot for clear answers. Johnny's been on his own for some time now—and something's not quite right."

Had I known that, there would have been no reason to feel alone and despondent. It seemed that Mike had everything under control from the Whereever side—especially since he'd maintained his quota of public farts. Glenn kept in touch as much as possible, which meant relaying intuitive messages when the long antennae of the Leprechauns weren't tuned in.

As it turns out, Larry had run into trouble when he tried to convince the other Recruiters that Barb and I should be accepted as Committeds. While we were both passable as individuals, *new* Committeds were always a liability—they thought too much about themselves, instead of apprenticing with their whole heart and soul. But Larry was glib enough to assure them that his judgment was sound.

After hearing this from Glenn, I became quite intrigued about the possibility that the other Recruiters would question Larry's decision. When we were scrunched around a smoky fire in the cave, I raised this very question and found that it reinforced my early morning idea. "You know fellas, if we can capture Larry, it'll *really* shake up the Leprechauns. Really, who but the most inept Leprechaun could get caught by a mere Human? And if we bag Brian too, we can *really* blow the lid off their Experiment!"

At the same time we were hatching our scheme in the cave, Mike—not knowing who was a real Leprechaun or near-hundred-percent apprentice—went about planning other kinds of sabotage. Oh, Mike was a clever one, I tell you.

Upon his return to Whereever, Mike cleverly started a conversation in one of the Shops about how wrong revenge was. "Imagine, *Group A* goofs up, and *Group B* gets so bent out of shape that they retaliate. Can you imagine such a *barbaric* reaction? I mean, if someone slips up, shouldn't they be forgiven?" Mike slipped this into a conversation so naturally that—when he farted to punctuate it—everyone accepted it as real.

His little performance was especially impressive because the blissfully carefree people of Whereever tended to think that anyone who retaliates for any reason is evil. Even so, the ultimate success of the adventure depended on excellent acting and perfect timing to trick and capture the Recruiters—after all, avoiding capture is one of the Leprechaun's greatest strengths.

Good move, Mike.

CHAPTER 27

▼

We discussed our strategies and carefully rehearsed our various roles. I was to be the sad, lost, and weary sinner who wanted to return to the fold. Glenn was to be the renegade who tried everything to be independent, but failed. Ben and Stan pretended to be mindless bumpkins, who are only capable of following a leader.

Of course, we couldn't all put on *Academy Award* performances simultaneously. That *would* have aroused suspicion. We finally decided to station Ben and Stan outside the cave for a couple of days to attract attention. We were counting on the idea that, when the Leprechaun patrol caught sight of them, the principal actors would take over. I was well aware that Larry's countryman, Bobby Burns the poet, had once written 'that the best laid plans of mice and men often go astray'—I think the Gaelic was something like *gang aft a-gley*. Well, we'd laid our trap, and now prayed that it wouldn't *gang a-gley*.

The sensitive Leprechauns finally picked up the out-of-the-cave Human vibrations. Naturally, they relayed the find to Larry.

"Grumpys," he said, wondering just which escapees had been located.

The scouts went back and returned with the names Ben Bow and Stan Lew.

"Lesser beings. Where is the *big fish,* Glenn Mye rhymes-with-eye?—Must be in the cave where it's too dense to locate him." After a thoughtful pause, Larry added, "Any sign of Johnny McMann yet?"

The success of the plan depended on two things. First, getting Larry to visit; and second, tricking him into manifesting into solid, physical form. We figured the first would be easy—after all, he is a Recruiter, and no one in that esteemed position wants to look bad. It was clearly of utmost importance for Larry to maintain his credibility in the eyes of the others, so we worked on his ego. The manifesting was a whole different ball game—our plan was for me to lead Larry back into the cave as he approached. Because he would have to become dense in order to find me there—that's when I would grab him.

After a few days, Glenn casually strolled out of the cave to make a showing. Once we knew the Leprechauns were onto us, we also knew they were drooling to get us back. After another few days, I peeked out—looking so forlorn that it was visually obvious that I missed my dear Barbara, and was tired of living with these heathen renegades....

Ben and Stan were blundering around the mouth of the cave like blind fools, while Glen acted as if he was on his last leg. My appearance as an incredibly forlorn and lovesick husband must have been perfect, because even the boys felt sorry for me. But my real act was *thinking*—because we knew that those Leprechaun antennae were picking up every thought and nuance. *'I so love and miss my sweet Barbara, the love of my life. I'll do anything to be back with her! Oh, Barbara, dear Barbara, pleeease....'*

It took awhile, but Larry and his cohorts picked up the vibes—and once they locked onto the signal, they looked like crows eying road-kill. But as much as Larry wanted to swoop in, he wisely contacted Mike McGee for verification. "Mike, lad, check them out—Grumpys are not to be trusted, even when forlorn." How we laughed inside—Mike verifying us! When Mike 'investigated us' and farted in the cave, we were barely able to control ourselves—it took great restraint to maintain our roles in the midst of silent laughter.

Mike's act was worthy of an *Oscar*—he laid it on so thick that Larry almost cried. He told Larry that we were so badly off that we were completely willing to return to Whereever and the Leprechaun Apprentice Program. Mike later reported that poor Larry swallowed the story hook, line, and sinker; especially when he told the Recruiter that we just didn't know of a dignified way to return. And perhaps, if Larry himself fetched us in physical form, the whole thing would be dramatically meaningful to every Leprechaun.

We pretended to be so distraught that we didn't notice Larry's approach. Meanwhile, each of us held submissive thoughts appropriate to the roles we were playing. I pulled my hair, moaned, and even pleaded, "Please, Larry, *help me*. I really want to become a Leprechaun, and with my wonderful wife Barbara, in Whereever."

As Larry approached, I retreated a few steps into the cave … though deep down, I was feeling, '*come to Papa—yes, come to Papa*….'

Once Larry was inside, I grabbed his hand while the others pounced on him—the ensuing scuffle was brief. The Leprechaun was so surprised that he just lay there in a daze, wondering what had actually happened. How else could it be after our masterful performances? And, who could understand what had just taken place besides us four desperados? We had outwitted and captured a real Leprechaun!

"Let me look at the rascal," said Ben.

"Not so high and mighty now, is he—look at the squirt now," added Stan.

"So," Glenn said majestically to our captive, "the brogue's on the other foot now, eh Larry?"

"I … I … I…."

"We know. You don't know what to say, nor what to think—or even do. We pulled the *ultimate* trickery, didn't we Larry? Ha!"

But I sensed the Wee One wasn't as helpless as he let on. I knew as well as I was sitting on his chest that his mind was going a hundred kilometers an hour. And sure enough, when he overcame the surprise and caught his breath, he began weaving a get-away plan.

"Great sport lads," Larry proclaimed, as he attempted to rise. "Aye, ya' certainly pulled a good one. Too bad I'm a bit out of shape—I might've given ya' more of a challenge a century or so ago. I say, lads, ya' must be a bit hungry with so little to eat out here—how about we go to the Village and have a bite?"

We were all half-starved, but in full possession of our senses. Keeping our plan foremost, we didn't allow ourselves to succumb to his golden tongue.

"Why certainly, Larry," I remarked. "We will definitely go to Whereever, and we'll gorge too. But, on *our* terms—is that clear?"

"Terms?" said Larry innocently. "Why lads, food is food, soft beds are comfortable, and a clean bath can't be beat. And happiness—why, doesn't that just take first prize! Aye, yer prank was a good one—but 'tis time to put a stop to all this nonsense. Just let me up so my tweeds won't get more soiled than they are."

No one moved. I held one wrist and Glenn the other, while Ben and Stan secured his ankles. Then, with dramatic gusto worthy of a *Grammy Award*, Mike brought closure to our success.

His gaseous report echoed wildly throughout the cave.

CHAPTER 28

▼

We had a good long talk with our captive, letting him know clearly that our purpose was to stop all plans for revenge—ideas that could lead to disaster. And they'd probably be worse for the Leprechauns in the long run.

Mike spoke first, in order to let the Recruiter know what side he was really on. "You see, Larry, we really are sorry for the way our ancestors treated you and yours. All that violence to the Wee Folk, destruction of your homes, and generally making the world inhospitable for Elementals—that was inappropriate. It must have been as humiliating as it was physically damaging. But Larry, that's the *past*. Again, it's unfortunate that it happened, but we don't want it to continue any more than you."

"That's right," added Glenn. "Can't you see that with you as our captive, we could cause *real* damage—but won't? We have the upper hand now, not you. Not one of your Recruiter friends will touch a Human as long as we have you. That means that we could walk into every one of your colonies and do anything at all, with no resistance."

"But we're not going to, *because that is not our purpose*," explained Stan. "We just want all of this Experimentation to stop. And to show that we don't want this conflict to continue, you—Larry—are going to stop it all. That's right, you're going to instruct the whole gang—Bascomb, Lung Chu, Pauul, Julio, Sidje, Ooma, and especially Brian—that the entire Experiment is *over and finished*."

"Isn't it ironic that we physical, dense, and unfeeling Humans aren't going to stop the Leprechaun Experiments by bashing a single house or tossing *even one* Leprechaun around. You should thank us for what we're about to do," said Ben.

I noticed that Larry pretended not to hear a word we said—it was clear that he still thought he could trick us and escape. "Gentlemen, Larry is not convinced that he is our eternal captive, and under our control forever. There is only one way to prove that we rule." I pulled a clam shell from my pocket. "A little souvenir from my honeymoon, though not a perfect shell."

Larry's eyes lit up. They didn't *twinkle* the same way they did when he was flirting or showing off—he knew what was coming.

Have I mentioned that Larry sported an orange beard? It was a tuft of hair that served as a goatee, but also acted as a Leprechaun *Badge of Honor*. I grabbed hold of it, and not gently....

The Wee One would have vanished instantly when threatened so severely, had he been *spirit*. But, being pinned to the ground, he was trapped in material form.

"What's with the shell, Johnny?" asked Glenn.

"Larry knows, don't you, lad?"

Leprechaun happiness is a glorious thing, and contagious. But their fear spreads hopelessness that tops that any day. Mike, Glenn, Ben and Stan felt nearly as desperate as Larry, as I held the clam shell in front of the Imp. "It's like this," I said to my friends, "you cannot bargain with a Leprechaun. That's a given—right, Larry?"

"We Humans can threaten, we can promise and say any number of things—but as long as they're only words or gestures, they go for naught. Right again, Larry? Well boys, the only way to deal with an Imp at *crunch time* is to act—and there you have it." With that, I tugged on his orange beard and unceremoniously sawed at it with the dull shell.

Those who have heard a captured pig squeal can understand one of the sounds Larry let loose across the countryside…. Those who have wrestled a crocodile can appreciate the thrashing that reverberated through the ground…. And those who have been close to a lightning strike can appreciate the horror that emanated from the wrist- and ankle-bound Leprechaun struggling against the four of us. But amazingly, the Imp simultaneously did all this and even more.

I'm not particularly proud to be the only one ever to shave off a Leprechaun's beard, but it had to be done—no matter how painful or humiliating. I knew it, and Larry knew it. And after it was over, the Grumpys knew that the only way to change a Leprechaun's attitude is to change his paradigm.

Larry lay limp—he had no will or strength left. All of us knew he'd lost his pride and power over us, and every Elemental who saw him would also know. He was like *Bald Samson of the Bible,* who also lost his great power with the shaving of his hair.

"You see, guys," I said, while drilling a hole through the shell, "action really does speak louder than words. Ten minutes ago, Larry was as powerful as any of his Race. Now, there's no need for the four of us to hold him. Being handcuffed to any one of us will keep him in check forever."

"It was still horrible," said Mike.

"Ghastly," added Glenn.

"Downright humiliating," said Ben.

"*And* inhumane," concluded Stan.

"But necessary," I emphasized. "Because now, all Recruiters will know that the game is over. Now they will *know* that we mean business, and that we are back in control of our own lives. Without this, the eternal tug of war between our Races would have continued. And as a result of our success, it may be that we can stop with Larry—for now, anyway."

After the clam shell was fastened around Larry's neck, I said officially, "Be it known that from this day forward, this is the only badge Larry Leprechaun will wear—*The Badge of Defeat.*"

Word of Larry's situation traveled through Leprechaun Land as fast as a thought. The Recruiters gathered and conferred; but one look at down-in-the-mouth prisoner Larry, and every Leprechaun knew he could only surrender. Brian's transformation was particularly impressive—one moment he was a King, and the next a powerless and ordinary Leprechaun. In the end, it turned out that we had managed to subdue both Leprechauns with one clam shell … and perhaps all of Leprechaundom itself!

The Leprechauns disbanded the Colonies and escorted all apprentices back to their earthly environments. The movement, which the Imps called *the Experiment*, was over. Never again would the Leprechauns try to weaken Man—and to insure that, we kept Larry handcuffed to one of us at all times.

Larry was our ace-in-the-hole against any future Experiments.

CHAPTER 29

▼

It didn't take long for the four of us to settle back into our normal Human lives. We'd had more than a taste of roughing it like Guerilla-Grumpys, so the hypnotic effect of the Leprechauns had worn off quickly. Some of the girls, Sally McGee and Susan Margoles especially, still giggled a lot and thought it cute to continue the bliss-ninny act. Even Barbara couldn't quite grasp why the good times had ceased. But the guys stuck together after the takeover, and we felt safe.

The surprise of the group was the trio of Mothers—Midge, Mary, and Penny. They moved in together on Elm Street and seemed to re-acclimate to real life quite easily. Midge's husband, Tory, naturally looked after them all. And the six children grounded the ladies, so they felt as if they'd only been on an extended vacation.

To make sure we all entered Human life and activity successfully, Mike, Glen, Ben, Stan, Ted Margoles and I played cards once a week, bowled another evening, and organized frequent backyard barbeques. Of course, the real reason for this was that no one wanted to be the exclusive lep-sitter for Larry.

So every time we held an event, we passed the handcuffs to a new Man. We decided to contain Larry long enough to make our point *absolutely clear*—but everyone knew we'd eventually free him. Our strategy was to hold onto him long enough that the other Leprechauns would believe that retaliation of any kind would be unsuccessful.

One evening after many months of celebrating our independence, we had a party in my backyard—and all the survivors of Larry's Whereever were there. As a group, we clearly overcompensated for our months of near-starvation by downing a keg of beer, grilling more steaks than there are counties in the longhorn-state, steaming enough corn on the cob to make the state of Iowa proud, and trying our best to finish off three giant watermelons.

As everyone relaxed and reminisced, we dragged Larry to the front.

"Well gang, we did it. We survived an experience probably no other Humans on earth have—except the inmates of the other Whereevers. Who has ever captured a Leprechaun before?" I raised my own hand, and the limp arm of Larry followed. "Am I the only one who believes that we don't have to continue to humiliate our guest any longer? What do you say—shall we let him loose?"

"I don't know," said Mike McGee. "He's a sly one, he is."

"True," added Glenn, "but smart, too. I suspect he's learned his lesson by now."

"So, should we release him?"

Poor Larry—he could only look at the ground. I doubt he heard a single word. *Just imagine an Extraordinary Leprechaun suddenly losing that status. No wonder he was drooped over with nary a twinkle in his eyes, humiliatingly shackled and beardless....*

In unison, everyone said, *"Free the bugger!"*

I looked at Larry and said as officially as possible, "Mr Lepricorn, you are now *free.*"

Most of us stood at the ready when the handcuffs were unlocked—especially the four Grumpys.

Larry looked up like a slave granted sudden and unexpected freedom—he didn't know what to say. We expected him to leap and bound and cast spells, or exact revenge on the spot. Instead, he only stood and stared.

"Go on Larry, you're *free.* You're no longer under Human control. No more dense brutes to manhandle you—be gone." I sensed that Larry thought we were just playing with him, and that we'd jump on him again, like a cat on a once-captured mouse.

"We're serious, Larry," said Mike. "You're free. But if you want to continue ... we'll let you stay longer. Johnny, the handcuffs...."

That's all it took—Larry's eyes lit up and the *twinkle* returned to his eyes. And with all the dignity he could muster, he removed the clam shell from his neck. "If ya' don't mind, Johnny McMann, I really don't need this or the 'cuffs as souvenirs to remind me of yer hospitality." He straightened up, quickly patted a few wrinkles out of his tweed suit, placed his tam squarely on his head, and dusted his brogues so they weren't completely scruffy. Then he took a deep breath, bowed, and vanished.

"Three cheers for Larry Lepricorn!" I yelled.

We all applauded, confident this was the last any of us would ever see Larry or any other Leprechaun again.

CHAPTER 30

▼

With Larry gone, we were now free of all Leprechaun influence, as well as the confinement of being constantly shackled to him. And what a freedom—we actually found the Human *grind* to be somewhat pleasurable. I found myself enjoying negotiations with customers, as well as the squabbles, and occasional disappointment of losing a client. It had never before occurred to me how frequently, and almost automatically, disputes seemed to occur—probably passing unnoticed because we're always so busy.

Sheila noticed the change in me during a price war over the Lewis Place, when I dove into the fray like an armed warrior. She whipped out her compact and prettied up in order to soften the blow with the client. To me, it just seemed like good, healthy sparring; but it took both of us awhile to re-adjust.

The other cavemen—Glenn, Ben, and Stan—had similar experiences. Ben, the salesman, dug into his customers like a prospector into a new gold mine. Glenn didn't shy away from any complaining worker in his contracting company. And in

Stan's landscaping business, he began suggesting to customers the best locations for planting trees and hedges. We all enjoyed every encounter.

The girls too, after overcoming their giggling, seemed to present a stronger front than before the *Whereever fiasco*—as they called it. Their increasingly frequent teas and coffees almost sounded like a debate room, rather than all the sweet talk they'd grown accustomed to at Whereever. So, it didn't take long for all of us to return to our common Human ways.

We were also pleasantly surprised when our increasingly bold stance brought more clients. It seemed that they wanted definite statements instead of roundabout approximations. And in the long run, the straight talk produced healthier business interactions, which promised a bright future for all of us.

The true sign of our assimilation, however, was when Mike McGee gave up letting farts in public.

Then, suddenly and quite unexpectedly, something interesting happened—life *without* Larry felt odd, and sort of *wrong*, as if we were missing something. It seemed as if he belonged *among* us, just not in Whereever. When we all expressed similar feelings, we wondered what hold the Leprechaun had on us.

"Nothing," said Mike openly. "I'm my own Man, as we all are. I think the only reason he enters our thoughts is because we're idealists with a predilection for fun. And no one can honestly say that Larry and Leprechauns in general, aren't fun when they're naturally themselves. That does not mean we're dependent upon them."

"Agreed," said Glenn. "When I build a house, it's always with the intention of creating a place that'll make the owner happy. But that's a Human trait, not a carryover from Leprechaun programming."

"I ditto that," concurred Stan. "A bower here, a flower bed there—it's always to make an estate the perfect place, which has always been *my* way of doing things."

"We're not as bound to Larry and his training as much as we fear we are. After all, Leprechauns don't have a monopoly on happiness," I added.

"I suppose you're right," added Ben Bow. "We're happy by nature. So when Larry came along and preached living in bliss forever in Leprechaun Land, we assumed *he* was the one creating the good times.... It seems that we're awfully susceptible to suggestion."

"You know what, boys? I wonder if, when you add all the parts, the sum is not only greater but also more interesting than the parts?"

"Uh oh," said Barbara, listening in. "You sound as if you're cooking up more than a barbeque. What's up?"

"Gather 'round. I have something wiggling away in my mind, and need to let it out before the thing burrows a hole in my skull."

"Sounds serious," said Barbara. "Girls, it looks like we're included in this scheme." All closed in.

"Ahem ... well, we've all come to some interesting conclusions recently—and, let's face it, we've all experienced something really extraordinary. If we didn't feel like escaped POW's right now, I think we'd all agree the experiences in

Whereever were basically good. So why not re-create Whereever ourselves, *Human style?*"

"You've got to be kidding, Johnny. Go back to Whereever and be Larry's pawns again?"

"*Never!* I mean that we all have several things in common—we've mentioned idealism, wanting to make people happy, and enjoying each other's company. So, look—why don't we make our bond more permanent?"

"We're listening."

"Well, I'm in real estate, Glenn Mye rhymes-with-eye is in construction, Stan 'scapes land—we're all in related fields. Why not pool our individual expertise to create our own concrete, both-feet-on-the-ground, Ideal Community—a place for *like-minded and eco-friendly people to be together?*"

The pause overshadowed the pungent odor of burning barbeque sauce.

"It would save trucking kids all over town," said Midge shyly.

"We could create our own Gathering any time we wanted," said another.

We were on a roll.

"I'll handle the land, Glenn supervises the building, Stan plants till he's green in the face, Ben sets up *real* Shops to sell from...."

"Don't think you have to do it all," said Susan. "Ted and I can add income that will help it float."

"Wow," said Barbara. "I hate to say it, but this sounds like Whereever—you know, the Ideal Community with everyone in his own Shop, but making money and socializing. What I can do is to start our own preschool and home school—Teddy, Colin, Amanda, Samantha, Beebee and Deedee can be my first students."

Another pause.

"You know," said Sally McGee, "there really wasn't anything *wrong* with the Shops at Whereever, except the Leprechaun thing. If we ran them—that is, from our own homes—and we socialized the way we do now with coffees and teas, none of it would be fake. It would be real … a real blast."

Many heads nodded.

"Well then, to get things started, I'll check out what land is available. Glenn can draw up plans for the units. Just one thing, though." Everyone looked up, anticipating a major problem.

"We need to give it a name—a real name. Any suggestions?"

CHAPTER 31

▼

The *Here and Now* Housing Addition was a success before the first brick was even laid. And it well should have been, since the twenty-two members had already lived together and become accustomed to one another. Our roll call was: Mike and Sally McGee, Glenn and Sissy Mye rhymes-with-eye, Stan and Janice Lew, Ben and Freeda Bow, Ted and Susan Margoles, Barbara and Johnny McMann, and Midge-Mary-Penny along with Tory and the six children. All in all, it was a very workable array of successful people.

A four-acre plot of land was located on the edge of town that looked ideal for our purposes. It abutted the county park in the rear, and on either side stood two estate homes. The word amongst realtors was that a mall might be put in across the road, and that's one reason I bought the land when the price was still low. It turned out that the mall did go in, so there was a great deal of construction going on in the west end of town for some time.

Glenn did a great job with the plans. He even made room in the center for a playground and community hall. Stan, with

142

a penchant for birch and willow, placed clumps of white trees throughout—and an enviously shaded willow bower at the edge of the park. But in spite of all the physical contributions that went into Here and Now, its success was assured by the underlying dedication, commitment, and vibrant *esprit de corps*.

On moving-in day, everyone naturally rejoiced and celebrated. We cut a giant ribbon, signed deeds, had a huge barbeque, and helped each other move. What a day! Only when I sat at my desk to put the events in my Journal did it hit me that exactly one year had passed since Larry Leprechaun had *popped* into my office and pulled his vanishing and desk-walking stunts.

And what Journal entries, too! Getting married, Larry and the entire Whereever thing, the Grumpys taking charge and capturing a Leprechaun, stopping a world-wide movement that could have emaciated all Humans, and now twenty-two of us living in a newly built housing development that we had created ourselves. As I read the entries, my reaction alternated between head-shaking and smiling. Occasionally, I'd wink at Barb, and she'd read over my shoulder and add her reactions.

Life at *Here and Now* became very special.

At the end of the first week, Sheila presented me with a schedule that opened my eyes wide. As in most businesses, success breeds success—but I wasn't prepared for what was coming our way. Several prominent residents—the owners of estates next to Here and Now—had watched the progress of their new neighbors' project. Being sound businessmen themselves, they passed the word among their wealthy friends. And before long, real estate people were knocking on our doors asking about plots, parcels, and how to attract the right kind of people. That week alone, I spoke to three groups that wanted to duplicate our *Utopia*.

The results of the meetings and the publicity caused a deluge of contracts to construct housing developments throughout the country. Interestingly, many investors told us that they particularly liked the paradigm underlying our project, where real down-to-earth, and like-minded people live together without barriers.

It was too long for a slogan, but the *'It's real'* captured their fancy.

CHAPTER 32

▼

In time, everyone who'd experienced the Leprechaun Experiment was both successful and happy. And it pleased us that this was all of our own doing. No hypnotism, no mass psychological programming, no revenge or evil motives.... We'd accomplished it all on our own, and were very proud of our achievements.

However, with all those recurring memories of Whereever and reminders from the Journal, everyone shared the conviction that the Leprechaun Experiment felt very real as it had happened ... *and Larry's presence was missed.* These feelings hung over each one of us—you might even say they haunted us.

One evening when everyone was gathered in the Community Center, I said something that drew as much response as my suggestion to build Here and Now had at first. The tone now was also very different.

"Are you *crazy*, Johnny? Invite the very Leprechaun who tried to fry our brains?"

"How can you think such a thing, Johnny? Larry and the Leprechauns led a dangerous conspiracy against us and *all Humanity*. Bringing him here would make us traitors and co-conspirators!"

"It's history, Johnny—*let it go!*"

After recoiling, I defended myself. "You guys are really getting bent out of shape. Don't you think I know the ramifications of the suggestion—but they're really unfounded. They only *sound* bad. First, Larry would never show his face again after his severe humiliation—unless he was thoroughly convinced we wouldn't harm him. Second, all Leprechauns know that if we can capture once, we can do it again. Which means neither side would even think of taking advantage of the other. Hey guys, the reason I suggest Larry—or even Brian and the other Recruiters for that matter—is as a gesture of goodwill. Bad feelings should not exist forever."

"*Goodwill?* Can you elaborate, Johnny, before we string you up by your thumbs?"

"Think about it," I replied confidently. "The Leprechauns have this notion that Humans are gross physical beasts, right? They're convinced that because their molecules are spread out, they're more *spirit* and also *superior,* right? Furthermore, they're positive that we're dumb-ugly-destroyers, while they're creators who have a monopoly on happiness."

"I get it," said Stan. "You're saying that we invite them here so they can see that their notions don't hold water. They learn that our violent overthrow was not because we're *intrinsically* violent, but because we want to be *our own people*—just the way they want to be pure Leprechauns."

"Now you've got it."

But the debate wasn't all on my side. Mike interjected, "Only a fool puts his hand on a hot stove a second time." Many heads nodded. To which Stan countered, "Yes, but give a sinner a second chance and he often redeems himself," which also nodded heads. "Give a tyrant an inch and he'll take a mile," drew approval. But it was balanced by, "Who says you can't teach an old dog a new trick—as long as you keep him on a *short* leash?" Back and forth went the words and clichés until Mary and Penny excused themselves to put the children to bed.

Sensing that some conclusion was needed, Stan summarized, "On our side, all's well and good since they know we can't be hoodwinked a second time, and will remain self-sovereign no matter what. From their side, Elementals have been hit hard throughout history, so that is forefront in their minds. I suspect they don't care even a bit about our self-sovereignty, and they'll *never* come around again. We all know that Leprechauns aren't stupid."

"So, how can we convince them that we're not going to attempt to annihilate them if they come?" inquired Ben.

"By example—show them that we're peaceful, loving, and happy. Demonstrate that we will not harm them even if we were inclined to. They need to know that we are, in fact, good peace-loving people at heart. In fact, I'd include in the invitation, 'Check us out *in spirit form*, psych out our thoughts and dreams—but at least check us out, because we do want to be friends.'"

"Hmmm …" responded Mike. "We could add that Humans like closure—'Let's settle our differences once and for all'."

"Sending invitations can't do any harm. *But how do we deliver them?*"

Chapter 33

At this time, Barbara—as wife and teacher, along with Mary and Penny—as Mothers, stepped in.

"Girls," announced my beautiful wife at tea time. "Enough of the testosterone approach. With all due respect to the greatness of Men, haven't we learned that it's the aggressive, macho, chest-beating attitude and approach that Leprechauns hate and fear the most? If Johnny's idea has any chance of success, it will only happen with a *feminine touch*."

"I agree," said Penny, straightening her apron. "My experience has been that Leprechauns love all that is naturally soft, gentle, and merry. Aren't those the very words that best describe Women—especially Mothers?"

"Yes," agreed Mary, fidgeting with her broad-rimmed bonnet. "But if we're not careful, we might cause *another* Leprechaun Experiment accidentally. By that, I mean that maybe we shouldn't even be thinking these thoughts unless the whole group is present. Who knows, maybe Larry is picking up on our thoughts right now. He's pretty sly, that one."

"True. They might think they can worm their way into the feminine heart, and thereby divide and conquer. We *should* be careful."

"Girls, girls," said Barbara. "Do you hear yourselves? Don't you remember how Larry looked when he was 'cuffed to the Grumpys—all shaven? He looked like the most defeated Leprechaun I've ever seen. Don't worry about any attempt to avenge us a second time. Believe me, Leprechauns are lovers at heart."

The women agreed to suggest to the entire group the idea of inviting the Leprechauns for a look-see, as long as everyone agreed to keep an eye on the Imps' every move—and thought.

"Fine," said Mary. "So let's say the men agree. What will be the mechanics of sending the message to the Wee Folk?"

CHAPTER 34

▼

To Bubbo, Whereever was not an experiment—it was part of his private plan for revenge. *He was actually the sole cause of the entire fiasco.*

Centuries before, Bubbo had been roughed up by Scottish Highlanders, who claimed that the Wee Folk had scared the farm beasts so much that they produced less milk and gave birth to runty calves. Bubbo, unlike most Leprechauns, gave vent to his feelings, not minding who heard him. "Ye' think you're high an' mighty Humans. But time'll come, I tell ya', when you're put down a notch 'r three. Aye, an' I may be the *verrry* one'll do it!"

"Well, laddie," challenged the Highlander Clan Chief, "what army will you hire to back up your threats? Be gone you runt, for you'll do nothing but bring more harm to all your folk!"

The Highlander added insult to injury by throwing cow dung at Bubbo.

Insulted, beaten, and insulted again by the meat-eating brutes was more than Bubbo could take. For years, the bile boiled within him, until it finally erupted like a volcano—then he took action. Bubbo had complained and talked, and complained more, until most of his fellow Leprechauns ignored him. Still, there were those few who followed the precept that 'the squeaky wheel should not be ignored'. And when the lad kept squeaking and squawking, they listened.

Leprechauns had been primarily solitary creatures before Bubbo presented his plan. Getting them all together was a bit against their nature in the first place. But enough of them went along with the revolutionary's plan to make a majority. And some joined his ranks just to shut the rabble rouser up. For several centuries more, the grouchy, irritable, red-bearded Imp quietly plotted his revenge and developed his plan of attack. Those who came forth to support Bubbo's plan had also been insulted by the brutish Humans—and had their homes leveled as well.

Stalwart Leprechauns stepped forward—lads known for their cunning, bravery, and leadership. First and foremost was Brian. At that time, he was known mostly for his purity and magnetic aura—and was considered a Prince among Leprechauns. It was Brian's subtle demeanor that Bubbo most admired, for it was this very trait he lacked entirely. Once Bubbo had Brian in his ranks—and proclaimed him King—others followed like sheep trailing their shepherd.

"The way to win, lads," said Bubbo in his inaugural pep talk, "is to keep the Experiment foremost in our minds at all times. Our plan is to slowly dilute the great density of a few Humans 'til they resemble Leprechauns. In this way, they'll become so changed that their fellow brutes'll barely recognize 'em. Then we spread the word that Leprechauns're great, and that all Men would do well to follow their friends' example. It's a masterful touch—we let the Humans destroy 'emselves!" Bubbo was banking on the premise that once an idea catches the imagination of a small percentage of Humans, the rest will blindly follow.

Bubbo was so convinced that weakening the brutish giants was the best way to avenge his roughing up, that he enlisted other leaders—Leprechauns close to the greatness of Brian. First came Bascomb, then Lung Chu, followed by Pauul, Julio, Sidje, Ooma, and Larry—Leprechauns known for their adeptness at playing mental games and manipulating another's thinking. Bubbo's propaganda machine operated smoothly long before the Experiment ever began.

Bubbo had planned for the first Human recruits to join his Experimental Colonies by the turn of the millennium, for he knew that superstitious Humans looked upon such times as propitious. "'Tis a perfect time to begin a new idea," said the self-proclaimed leader. "Aye, the brutes're most susceptible when a century or millennium changes. So, we'll find the most idealistic an' promise 'em a better world—one of peace, love, happiness an' all those platitudes they swallow so easily."

Bubbo put his plan into action and his Ideal Whereever Villages filled and flourished.

To the average even-minded Leprechaun, the entire operation was seen as *an adventure and an experiment.* The Wee Ones were not into revenge at all. Moreover, they were confident that Humans were so dense that the few who might apprentice in Whereever would number enough to alter the rest of Mankind. This logic allowed many Leprechauns to accept Bubbo's plan.

But there were others who didn't trust the self-proclaimed leader at all. "Know this, Bubbo. If you and your Recruiters fail—that is, if the Experiment backfires and the brutes hurt a single Leprechaun—it will be the end of any possible Elemental-Human relationship forever. That would not be good, so beware that the crushing weight of failure may fall on your head, and *yours alone.*"

That's exactly what happened when the four Grumpys—myself, Glenn Mye rhymes-with-eye, Ben Bow, and Stan Lew—with the help of clever Mike McGee—captured Larry and exerted our will. Down went Bubbo, and back to their solitary lives went the Leprechauns. Moreover, the Elementals knew that they might never deal with Humans again. To protect themselves, the Leprechauns had concluded that Man and Leprechaun—being two different Races—would, should, and must, live separately. Well, *most of them had....*

But Leprechauns, being eternally curious, could never actually pull their feelers in all the way. So when they sensed that the *Here and Now* group was successful, some of them quietly scouted about—and the more daring even visited. These scouts went invisibly, with their molecules so spread out that even the most refined Human probably wouldn't be able to identify them. It was spying on the *spirit* level.

After the termination of the Experiment and all the Whereevers, the skeptical Leprechauns who had warned Bubbo exiled the Imp to the bramble bushes of *Nowhere*. It was so far distant and solitary that no one knew where he was.

And Larry was so humiliated that it took him seven hundred Leprechaun years to grow back his orange goatee. Even when the fuzz looked respectable enough to present in public, the poor fellow walked with so definite a stoop that he could see only the ground in front of him.

Because of their isolation, neither Bubbo nor Larry was aware that a few Humans in Here and Now were suggesting a peaceful relationship between Man and Leprechaun. And even if he'd heard, Larry was so demoralized that he wouldn't have been capable of doing anything.

As the founders of Here and Now thought more and more about reuniting with the Elementals, a few adventurous Leprechauns picked up on it. The idea slowly filtered through Leprechaun *spirit-consciousness.* So all of them knew about it—but so what? No Leprechaun in his right mind would *ever* be foolish enough to associate with Humans again. The idea of reconciliation did, however, float around.

The news even reached Larry—but humiliated and full of fear, the Wee One did his best to ignore it. That was rather easy, since his nature was actually shy and reclusive—and his delicate heart desired never to be hurt. Yet Larry, being a true Leprechaun, could not totally avoid every miniscule, nano-ripple of curiosity.

Finally, one of his pointed ears perked up.

CHAPTER 35

▼

After all that he'd been through, Larry wasn't about to make the same mistake again—he was no fool. So he categorically refused to even hover above Here and Now—no matter how invisible or diffuse his molecules. He even cringed when he picked up on fellow Leprechaun observations about the Community. Nevertheless, he was instinctively drawn to the Humans' noble effort to replicate Whereever as Here and Now.

When Larry heard that several of the ladies—Susan, Sally, Midge, Mary, and Penny were thinking of him, he almost smiled. He reminisced—*'Lady Humans can be sweet. Their hearts are purer than their male counterparts because they're not quite as dense. Aye, and they're also less aggressive. 'Tis nice they have me on their minds—but they're still Human ... and married to Men.'* Larry's entire body shuddered at the word 'Men'—and the memories that came along with it.

Over the Leprechaun centuries—which are truly not at all the same length as Man's—Larry had Committed to a fair Leprechaun named Lucy. And whenever he began complaining about Humans, she would coyly say, "Why Larry, if you talk like that, it'll boost your growth. Lands sake, you don't want to look like the very ones you begrudge now, do you?" Larry married Lucy because she was special, and was able to put everything in perspective.

"Besides," she added, "is there even the *weeist* chance the Giants aren't as bad as you say? And maybe the reason they laid hands on you was because ... well ... of something in you?" It was a daring thought, and only one as sweet as Lucy could have suggested it. When Larry didn't disappear from the universe at its utterance, Lucy knew she had spoken the truth.

"Whaddya' mean Lucy, something in me?"

"Now I'm only suggesting, that maybe one reason the Grumpys captured you was because you listened to their trickery *as if it were real.* Maybe—and I'm saying maybe—if you weren't so tricky yourself, then possibly you wouldn't have been so susceptible."

"I've heard that notion, dear. But ya' forget—in spite of how I was captured, they did the unpardonable act of desecrating my honor. Only the most despicable creature would even *think* of such a thing."

Normally, Larry was a fine fellow, calm and peaceful to the core. The fact that this one thing set him off so much caused Lucy wonder. *'Now, if this isn't a case of it taking a thorn to remove another thorn, then I don't know what is. My dear Larry is a Leprechaun through and through, so 'tis an absolute shame that he should walk through life with this Shadow of Shame on his soul. Oh, I do wonder if there isn't a way to rid him of this great burden—hate and fear are ugly things to have smoldering in your heart.'*

Lucy possessed not only a fine sense of perspective, but she also liked to set things straight. Aye, no sooner had she reflected about ridding her Committed of his deep despair, than she thought of Brian—*'Aye, everyone loves and respects the King. And no matter what the Humans think, Brian was a Recruiter and an Exhalted One.'*

With that, Lucy decided to contact Brian.

"A matter of self-esteem, and being able to live with yourself, is it not, Brian? My Larry's soul is noble and his heart so pure. It sours our very existence that a single one of us should carry such a burden—especially one as grand and glorious as Larry. What, O my King, can we do?"

"'Tis natural that you should want to help your Committed," answered Brian. "But you should know, Lucy, that he's been hit like no other Leprechaun in our eternal history. True, a few—but a very, very few—have had Humans lay hands on them, but they were always able to escape. Your Larry has done what he considers the single worst crime a Leprechaun can commit. Aye—and not once, but twice. Remember also that before the cave incident, he also let Johnny McMann slug him, he did."

"A sad affair, indeed," said Lucy. But she wasn't going to be overcome by crying. "Knowing all this, Brian, you must have *some* idea what we can do to set things straight?"

"Hmmm," reflected Brian. "You are persistent. All right then—what I propose is that we approach it indirectly."

"Beg'n' your pardon, Highness?"

"I mean, address the problem in a different way—*sort of through the back door.*"

"You mean to ignore it all, and let my poor Larry suffer through eternity? Ah Brian, you're too noble to let time heal this, seein' as how I want to settle it now. You do have something in mind, don't you?"

"Well, Lucy," prompted Brian, "do you remember Sean and Sarah Lowrey who lived in Larry's Whereever?"

"I do. Larry and the others thought they were a bit dull."

"Aye. And because of it, they were obliged to leave, right?"

"I believe so. And no one knows where they went."

"Well then," smiled the King. "Have you put two and two together yet?"

As Lucy thought, her Leprechaun eyes began to *twinkle*. "Are you suggesting that Sean and Sarah sneak through someone's back door and perform trickery?"

"Aye—and the door would be Johnny McMann's, in his own *Here and Now* Housing Development. The Lowreys could go as observers, don't you see? No one would ever suspect them, being so dull and all."

"But how could the Lowreys ever get in? The Humans can't invite them, since they don't know where they live."

"Well, Lucy, we arrange for Sean to bump into one of the residents of Johnny's Village. Accidentally, of course—perhaps somewhere in their town. He and Sarah can tell the group they were so dense that they couldn't pass test number one—and Larry kicked them out."

"I suspect the Humans will believe that," said Lucy.

"Aye, and my guess is that the gullible Humans will feel sorry for them, and accept them into Here and Now on the spot."

"Clever," said Lucy, smiling. "And once there, we'll know everything Johnny and his group are up to."

"Quite so. And knowing what they're up to, we'll know how sincere they are about giving up their infernal violence and making amends."

"Clever indeed," said Lucy, smiling even more broadly. "And the Humans won't suspect a thing because it's all round-about. But, then what?"

"Who's to say?" answered Brian in the confident manner of a leader. "That will depend on what Sean and Sarah find out. For all we know, the Here and Now folks are brewing revenge. So, we'll just have to see what our spies discover before we can decide on the next step."

CHAPTER 36

▼

Sean and Sarah Lowrey weren't actually dull—they were merely more low-key than most. They were what Humans might call a typical 'out-to-lunch' mentality. But compared to the average Man's hyperactive, finger-in-a-light-socket nature, the Lowreys *were* dull. The truth is that S and S had their fun and their own mischievous ways, though a Human would never guess it from their demeanor. Knowing that they were perceived this way, Brian and Lucy set the stage by making Sean an accountant, and Sarah a stay-at-home housewife and occasional painter.

"So, Brian," said Lucy, "I understand that the purpose of using the Lowreys in Here and Now is to provide inside information. But tell me, how will this soften Larry and strengthen his self esteem?"

"Ah Lucy, 'tis like playing chess, this strategy. The successful player must think several steps ahead. For this plan to succeed, two things need to happen simultaneously. As the Humans sympathize with Sean and Sarah, their acceptance will be automatic. Then, if the Lowreys report back that the

Humans are sincere about inviting Leprechauns as a way of healing past wounds, we slowly leak it back to Larry. That's true back-door strategy. Front-door would be to tell him outright. And we know that he would scream and yell at the likes of that."

"Anyway, if Larry hears *from fellow Leprechauns he trusts* that the Humans are truly sorry for what they did … that they did it only in order to save their Race … *and* that they're ready to apologize … then we just add in that they felt the only way to be free was to overpower him. In this way, Larry may be able to ignore their attack on him."

"You're a genius, my King," exclaimed Lucy.

"Hopefully," continued Brian, "we will have planted enough seeds in Larry's mind that he will at least *think* about visiting Here and Now—invisibly and all spaced out, of course. If the Lowreys have reported accurately, then your noble Committed should see a Race he *might* think worthy of approaching."

Lucy shook her head. "'Tis too much for me, this chess game you have in your royal mind, Brian—back door, front door, spies, invisible visits. I feel 'tis not chess we're playing, but some game of super-secret-agent straight out of a Human movie or TV program."

When Brian revealed his thoughts to his fellow Leprechauns, they applauded and Lucy felt much better.

"Brilliant!" some said.

"Splendid!" others agreed.

"Jolly good!" applauded more.

Everyone praised the plan. When they suggested it to Sean and Sarah, the two quite typically shrugged. All Sean said was, "No one wants to see a fellow down at the mouth. Sarah and I have nothing planned, so—why not?"

Sean dressed like an accountant and strolled into *Hokey's*—the coffee house frequented by the former Grumpys.

"Look, Mike, isn't that Sean—of Sean and Sarah Lowrey?"

"I think so. What's he doing here?"

"*Sean Lowrey*—hey, remember me, Johnny McMann? Why, I haven't seen you since ... since I last saw you."

"Yes, and it's been awhile," answered Sean in his dull voice. "Fancy meeting you here."

"Well, Sean, where'd you disappear to anyway? One day you and Sarah were there in Whereever—and the next you weren't."

Sean instantly picked up on my desire to know if he was a Leprechaun or Human. "Yes, it all happened so suddenly. One day we were respectable apprentices, and the next we were moving to Idaho. It seems that Larry finally gave up on us—you know, too dense to pass even the first test—so he escorted us back to Idaho. It was a bit of a let-down. Anyway, what about you and Barbara?" Everything Sean said was a ploy, since he'd done his homework. He already knew everything about all the residents of Here and Now, but had to work his way in naturally.

"Fit as fiddles," I answered, not suspecting a thing. "Say, do you know these fellas?"

"Can't say that I do. Hey—hello, I'm Sean. Johnny and I used to live in the same ... town."

"It's all right, Sean. They lived in Whereever too—but before our time, of course. They're the Grumpys we used to hear about."

"Grumpys? My, so you and Barbara aren't alone then?" He sucked me in expertly.

I retold the tales of the Cave, the Humiliation of Larry, and Dissolution of the Experiment.

Sean just shook his head. "Frankly, I'm glad I missed it all. Sounds so … so unsettling. As for us, Sarah and I are a bit unsettled ourselves. We're thinking of leaving Idaho because it's too cold, and would like to move somewhere warmer and more friendly. Say, are there any good jobs available here?"

Not one of the former Grumpys suspected a thing. In fact, we were so hospitable that we invited the Leprechaun actor to Here and Now, and even suggested that he work in my real estate business. Sean played his role perfectly—but that's not surprising, since trickery surges powerfully through a Leprechaun's very heart.

In a very short time, Sean became my accountant. Sarah did house cleaning in Here and Now, and also enjoyed painting. The Lowreys hugged old friends, ate at the local bar-beques, played euchre and cribbage in the Community Center, and chatted intimately with all of us—as if we were all still at Whereever. The whole charade had been so easy.

Sarah was in on the game too, of course. In her dull down-home way, she pumped the others with her questions. She would quietly ask how each friend got to Here and Now, and then entice them to reveal all the details. Each chimed in with his or her version of Whereever—one thought it was

Heaven, another so-so, while the majority loved the socializing.

One day when they were all gathered in the Community Center, Sarah asked quietly, in a hushed voice, "I wonder if Leprechauns and Humans will ever be able to get along?"

Glenn Mye rhymes-with-eye perked up, "Get along? I see no problem as long as neither sticks his nose in the other's business. Living *with* one another though—I doubt that because of our big differences."

"Maybe living *near* one another," suggested Ben Bow. "But that'd depend on us overcoming the feeling that they're always about to pull a trick on us. And them feeling we're about to crush them. That's two pretty big 'ifs'."

"I think everything would work out under those conditions," commented Mike. "After all, both Races like to be happy."

"Bravo! As long as nothing's fake—no con jobs, no brainwashing, no tricks."

"I have a feeling," said Sarah, "that you fellows have talked this out before. Especially the ones who call yourselves 'Grumpys'. Personally—and I'm speaking as one who's been away from them a long time now—it almost seems worthwhile to invite some Leprechauns here. You know, just to see how everyone reacts. Who knows, they might be thinking along the same lines we are."

"The truth is, Sarah," said Sally McGee. "That we've been sending out *vibes,* the kind Leprechauns pick up psychically."

"You've been sending them messages?" Sarah asked innocently, and with convincing astonishment. "Have they

answered? I mean—who would respond if their leader had been tackled, handcuffed, shaved, and his whole operation broken up? I'd be downright wary for sure, and definitely scared. Have you heard anything from them?"

"Nothing," said Freeda. "Not that we can blame them—but we *are* sincere."

"That's right," said Janice, licking her barbeque covered fingers. "We'd like to live in harmony, or at least be friends. Maybe it wouldn't amount to much more than a truce, but at least neither side would hold a grudge."

Then Sarah dropped another wordy bombshell. "I wonder, you know, whether Larry will *ever* change? He must've felt terribly shamed after being captured. But I do wonder if there's anything that could be done to encourage him to come forth and, well—deal with it." Sarah Lowrey was superb, playing her hand as if she held every trump card.

The group didn't pursue her comment. Instead, they cleaned tables and retired the charcoal. *But in their minds, the thought had acted like a flame to dry kindling.*

"You know, guys," said Barbara, "for all the wishing and hoping, our plan hasn't worked. Why not do what *has* worked?"

"And what might that be?"

"Mike McGee and Glenn Mye rhymes-with-eye."

"Mike and Glenn?" asked Sean, fully aware of the double-agent role Mike had played. "What did they do that worked?"

"I don't know—they never told us." Then, looking at my former Whereever neighbors and cave dwellers, I added, "hey guys—do you think you could use the same system now to contact the Leprechauns?"

"You *communicated* with the Leprechauns, Mike?" Sarah inquired, in her most innocently astonished voice.

"And you *talked with them?*" she asked Glenn. A shrewd onlooker might have been suspicious, but her melodramatic voice went unnoticed since everyone was thinking hard.

Glenn and Mike exchanged looks—and both smiled.

"Well, Mike," said Mr Mye rhymes-with-eye. "I'll give it a try as long as you don't revert to farting."

CHAPTER 37

▼

After Larry Leprechaun—*aka* Lawrence Lepricorn—had disgraced his Race by allowing himself to be slugged and then caught by Humans, he holed up in the most inhospitable thorn bush known to Elementals. Had it not been for Lucy, he would certainly have become so irritable and reclusive that he might've even turned into a thorn bush himself. Ashamed and humiliated, the Wee One didn't want to communicate with a soul, living or dead. That is, except for Lucy, whom he asked for porridge and a pipe now and again.

Lucy knew that at such a desperate hour, compassionate strength was the only possible way to reach her dear Committed. So she approached him with a full heart, saying, "Larry dear, eternity is a long time to pout, is it not? And just between you and me, and infinity—and all the stars above, I'll live with my dear one no matter how he feels. However, 'twould be much jollier if you were the *twinkle-eyed* Leprechaun of my Committment. What do you think of this idea to lift your *spirits,* dear—that you and I take a vacation and have a second honeymoon?"

"*Where in the glade did that come from?* I've no time to sport about. I have things on my mind!"

"Dearest Larry, time's exactly what you *do* have, and in abundance. I'd be as lowly as a Human to let my Committed wallow through his trials and tribulations alone, don't you see? So I've come to this, my dear *Sprite....*"

"Ye' say you've '*come to this*'?" shot back Larry, irritably. "Well lassie, I've come to *this*," and he burrowed deeper into his thorny dwelling.

"As I was saying, dear," persisted Lucy. "A decision's been made, it has, and I'm taking a vacation—with or without you. And if that doesn't *twinkle* your Committed vows, so be it." Concluding that a desperate time demands a desperate response, Lucy added, "which is to say that if you won't escort me—as all good Committeds should—I'll ask Brian to do the honors. He's most respected, he is, so there'll be only a minimum of gossip."

"*Zounds!* How ya' lack feeling for yer castaway Committed when he's down! And all the while, I've been thinking ya' were my eternally loving partner."

"I am that, my love—and 'tis the very reason I'm asking you to travel with me. Aye, to lift your *spirits* so you'll be the jolly, *twinkling* Sprite of old—the one I fell in love with, the one.... Aye, but that's up to you."

"Oh squelch it, *will ya'*. Ye' know I can't go anywhere without...."

"I've taken your loss of honor into consideration, sweetheart. Here, take these." And she handed him a set of false whiskers she'd picked up at a costume shop. "Wear this, and no one will recognize you. Now just come out of that thorn patch and we'll head out."

"*Twee Wee!*—I'm disgraced whether I come or go."

"To be sure—so, which is the lesser disgrace, to stay holed up knowing your Committed is out with another Leprechaun, or to put on that beard and come with me?"

CHAPTER 38

▼

What does a Leprechaun couple do on vacation?—not the same as a group of un-Committed rogues causing havoc every which way they turn, that's for sure! One story has it that such a wild group got it into their wee heads to follow the shoreline of every continent, half going right and the other half left. The winners, of course, would be everyone who reached the starting point. So off they went, and before *two twinkles,* they crossed paths at the tip of South America. And oh, how the lads leapt and bounded and skidded and scooted, so happy they were to see one another again! But all the rollicking upset the very oceans, causing the winds to blow in every direction, and the currents to be confused. The waves at Cape Horn were so turbulent they haven't yet recovered from that prank.

Oh no, that's not how a Committed couple spends a vacation at all!

For their second honeymoon, Lucy—trying her best to be the epitome of gaiety—urged her Committed to the South Seas, over the Alps, past the Mediterranean, around the coast of Australia, high over the Himalayas, around the warm

Hawaiian beaches, onto California, and dancing and prancing about the Highlands of Scotland. Oh, Lucy took him all over the earth, she did. Larry, of course, went incognito—hoping his false beard would cover his low *spirits* as well as his Leprechaun chin.

And Larry did his best to grumble at nearly every sight—at least during the first half of their vacation. But the more they traveled, the higher Larry's *spirits* climbed, contradicting how humble and grouchy he wanted to appear. By the time they hovered over the California beaches, Larry almost forgot he was wearing false whiskers, and began dancing a jig with some suntanned beauties. When he and Lucy sailed over the Highlands and heard the wonderful sounds of a lone lad playing the bagpipes to a herd of cows—which he pronounced *coos*—the Leprechaun was as good as cured.

As good as cured—but not quite completely. For, when they set their wee feet on the ground near their home in John O'Groats, Larry's gloom threatened to return. Ah, how quickly that bright mood and *twinkle* in the eye clouded over and began to retreat!

But Lucy was no ordinary Committed, and was doing everything she could to raise Larry's *spirits*. She felt his reaction even before he did, and telepathically relayed to her friends that it would be good to throw a festive Welcome Home Party for them. With all the gaiety and partying, even Larry couldn't continue to be gloomy, what with all the questions, back-slapping, and merriment.

The vacation had been a great success, and Larry was out of the *grumps* and nearly ready to resume normal Leprechaun life.

CHAPTER 39

▼

After the whirlwind vacation and Welcome Home greetings, Larry was feeling confident and full of himself. His *spirits* and *twinkle* had returned—a welcome transformation that was noticed by all.

Brian spoke casually about Here and Now—but his indirect approach was addressed to all Leprechauns, not only Larry. Indeed, Brian began planting the seeds of his plan ever-so-subtly while Larry was feeling good, knowing that it would have been a waste of time and energy if he'd had to overcome Larry's low *spirits*.

"Funny thing," observed the King, as if innocently observing the wind or the waves. "Word is that some Humans—former residents of Whereever—have built an Ideal Village and are living there together. Apparently, they were so impressed by our Whereevers that they decided to create their own version—and named it *Here and Now.*"

Others picked up on the idea before Larry could react verbally.

"*Really, Brian*—complete with Shops and socializing and all? *Well!*—Shows, doesn't it, that we did some good, no matter how it turned out," proclaimed Bascomb.

"I heard the likes," chimed in Pauul. "They so liked our system that they're copying it. Might be a place to cruise over sometime—like on a vacation."

"Oh, too bad we didn't know about it, Larry," chimed in Lucy. "We could have taken a look-see on our way back."

"Hmm," reflected Julio. "Interesting ... kind of piques the curiosity, doesn't it? I wonder what the Human version of a Gathering is like."

The whole discussion happened so naturally and subtly that Larry couldn't keep himself from feeling good. The inquisitive tone was sure to seep into every pore of his naturally curious Leprechaun nature.

CHAPTER 40

▼

The whole strategy was a set-up, of course. On the Leprechaun side, Lucy and Brian were softening up Larry. And on the Human side, the Lowreys were working on the Here and Now residents, who were sending their own messages of goodwill—also with the help of the Lowrey moles. But no one other than Brian and Lucy—and the Lowreys—knew what was really going on.

After all the positioning of both Races, it might appear that it was just a matter of time before they would meet again. Even so, the subtle preparations and waiting made the air prickle with anxious expectation.

If either side sensed trickery, everyone would have retreated—or vanished.

Mike McGee and Glenn Mye rhymes-with-eye had developed a good system for communicating between themselves in Whereever and the cave. But it didn't extend beyond them, no matter what they thought. Unbeknownst to the two, all contact was actually being managed between Sean and Sarah, and

Lucy and Brian. Of course, the Leprechauns naturally supported the idea that Mike and Glenn were doing it all.

So, while Mike continued his work of trying to communicate with the Leprechauns—wondering all the time if he was being successful—Sean and his Committed actually did the quiet work of relaying the activities and desires of Here and Now residents. Meanwhile, Lucy and Brian continued systematically planting more and more seed ideas in the garden of Larry's curious mind.

My jaw dropped when Jenny Oliver suddenly entered the Community Center— *"What, a spy?"*

"Spy my eye!" parried Jenny, smiling in her naturally coy way.

"And what kind of a greeting is that?" she countered. "I heard through the real estate grapevine that a group had created a special housing development. The agent was listed as Johnny McMann—and I just had to see for myself. Small world, isn't it?"

"Careful, boys, she's a true-blue Leprechaun if ever I saw one."

"Then you've never seen one," responded Sarah, as she hugged Jenny.

Indeed, it was Leprechaun Jenny who had telepathically suggested to Brian that—with her help—they could speed up Larry's healing.

"Jenny dear," continued Sarah, "is as Human as the rest of us. If you don't believe me, Johnny, why don't *you* hug her and see for yourself." Oh, that dull one knew Human psychology, she did.

It was an awkward moment—I wanted to hug her, but had to put up a good front. "Of course Jenny's dense, though the word *physical* is more accurate," I replied. "And, I prefer to shake her hand—if you don't mind. That is, if Jenny promises not to zip me off to Never-Never Land."

"If I'm not mistaken, sir, only a Leprechaun can do that—and a strong one to boot. Now, if you had your eyes wide open, you'd have known that I'm in real estate, just as you are. Solid, real, and down-to-earth—not the flaky stuff of Leprechauns and Faeries. Now quit being so skeptical—and prudish—and give me a real earthly hug."

That was more like it—either Jenny was a great Leprechaun actress, or she really was Human. Since there was no time to prove either case, we hugged one another as her beautiful body closed in on me. "Physical indeed," I confessed with a smile. "But clear something up for me. At Whereever, you were the Leprechaun of Leprechauns. How do you explain that?"

"Really, Johnny? Perhaps—like Mike here—I wanted everyone to *think* I was a Leprechaun." Her wink was as good as the Judge's gavel—*case closed.*

"Well, Jenny," said Sarah, like a good undercover agent, "now that we have that settled, I must admit that you had us fooled too. I would have sworn that you were a Leprechaun spy, here to check things out and keep an eye on us to see how we're progressing with our version of Whereever."

"It appears to me," said Jenny with mock sincerity, "that I should go into acting. Or, how about espionage?" Then, turning serious, she added, "although I prefer to stay in my own back yard—real estate. I'd rather sell parcels and plots of land than secret information."

Finally convinced, I hugged her again.

Although she didn't need to, Jenny further cemented her credibility by adding, "It's good to be back with familiar, smiling faces. After the break-up of Whereever, I returned to Omaha. With all respect for my hometown, I just couldn't settle down, because nothing was the same after being with all of you. Oh, I'm so glad I came across news of your development. Who's here from Whereever, anyway?"

She didn't need to say that either, because she already knew.

Since it was suppertime and everyone felt joyful, a potluck quickly emerged. No one noticed that the newest arrival didn't actually eat her food—she spooned and forked it around her plate as its essence was absorbed and the food silently vanished.

Jenny's presence was no accident, of course. The whole scheme had been well-planned and executed. The Leprechaun intent was to make Here and Now very successful, and such a likeness of Faerie-like Whereever, that neither Leprechaun nor former apprentice could resist checking it out—Larry included.

As Jenny settled in and established herself in her new home, and as the Lowreys became permanent residents, their reports back to Brian seemed happier and more optimistic. To squelch any remaining doubts concerning Jenny's true identity, she joined Johnny's real estate business and worked as hard as the best of them.

Everything was set.

CHAPTER 41

▼

The setup was better than anyone could have imagined.

One day during a meeting, while Larry was sitting quietly in the corner pretending not to be listening, Brian casually started talking about Here and Now. "Guess who's spying at Here and Now—the Lowreys *and* Jenny Oliver!"

Larry's little ears instantly perked up.

"Jenny *spying?*" asked Larry cautiously. "What for, if I may ask?"

"For the sake of spying," said Brian evasively, hoping Larry would swallow the whole bait. "Why else?"

"You've got me there, Brian."

But before the eavesdropper could continue the conversation, Brian spoke to the others in a staged whisper. "It seems that this Here and Now Village, the one these old apprentices have developed, has caught the imaginations of many. I mean, if you're going to live in a group, why not an *ideal* group? My fellow Leprechauns, do you know that we actually did these Humans a *favor* with our Experiment? They *liked* living together in Whereever, and became so accustomed to it that they've created Here and Now to continue the tradition!"

"What's this?" sputtered Larry, who never wanted to be the last one to hear the latest gossip. In his attempt to ignore the subject, he really had blanked out most of the chatter around him. But now, his curiosity was piqued—*"Something's going on,"* he stated, almost accusingly.

"'Tis nothing," said Brian offhandedly, "merely a bunch of former apprentices—and Grumpys—living together. That's all."

"Really …?" asked Larry. When he heard the word 'Grumpy', it made him swallow the bait a little bit deeper. "Jenny's there—and Sean and Sarah? Have they found out if the Humans are trying an Experiment of their own?"

"Good gracious, *no!*" interjected Lucy. She wanted the conversation to stop short of becoming serious. "Do you really think they're capable of the likes, my love?"

Larry didn't know what to believe.

"Dear," continued Lucy, in an undertone, "I can't fault your feelings for what happened. But the truth is that Johnny McMann, Glenn Mye rhymes-with-eye … and a dozen or so, I hear…. They're kind of duplicating Whereever—only Human *style*. Jenny and the Lowreys, bless their Leprechaun souls, are just curious and want to see what's going on."

Then she set the hook, "And I've half a mind to satisfy my own curiosity about it."

No one should ever believe that male Leprechauns have a monopoly on cleverness.

"Not without *me*, ya' won't," snapped Larry, totally unaware of how he was being manipulated. "What if they lay hands on ya' and shave *yer* head bald!"

It was an unthinkable idea, and everyone gasped—and *oohed* and *ahhed*. Such actors, the Leprechauns!

"Larry," said Brian quickly, "it's time for you to rid yourself of prejudices—quit scaring us with such violent words. No one said Humans are perfect. Just because they did what they did at Whereever doesn't mean they can't be kind-hearted. And according to Jenny, that's what they're doing at Here and Now. Besides, even if your dear Committed made herself invisible and spread out.…"

Larry sat in silence. He never wanted to think about Humans again, yet his Committed was forcing his hand.

Catching the moment and speaking ever so sincerely, Lucy said, "You know dear, I wouldn't go to the Humans in any form if you said 'no', even if Brian his-royal-self promised to protect me. But, you know what? I sincerely believe that if any Leprechaun is going to check to see if Jenny, Sean, and Sarah's reports are true, it should be you. Heaven knows you would give the single most objective report any Leprechaun could ever give!"

It was a masterful touch, and it took Larry by surprise. He had been led to the finish line so successfully that he actually wanted to get involved.

"You've been talking up this addition like it's really something," he said, puffing himself up in his tweed suit, cocking his head, and adjusting his tam-o'-shanter. "And truth be known, it *has* aroused my curiosity. Moreover, ya' know I despise second-hand reports and opinions. So, yes … perhaps I'll reconnoiter this Here and Now place. But ya' can bet John O'Groats and the very Highlands that the Humans will see nary a hair of me!"

CHAPTER 42

▼

My pensive silence ended with a reflective question, "What about the residents of the other Experimental Whereevers, the ones that I toured when you stayed back?"

"Other Whereevers?" asked Barbara with surprise.

"But Barb, don't you remember when Larry and I took that long Tour—when you stayed behind?"

"*Oh my goodness* ... the others had totally slipped my mind," she added, pausing in embarrassment.

"Yes ... yes, but everyone kept me so busy going from Shop to Shop. And Larry himself *popped* in so encouragingly, as if to keep me company. It almost seemed like he was trying to distract me."

"Indeed, but now seems like the time to reveal what I learned. You see, there are a lot of others out there who are in the same situation we're in. And now that we've established Here and Now, maybe we can help them."

"A lot of others? How many settlements were there, anyway?"

"Uh ... er...." I hemmed and hawed, not being able to remember exactly.

"Johnny, the Larry Log. That's the most complete record we have. And you kept it so painstakingly—and against Larry's wishes."

That's when I pulled out my Journal.

"Dear," said Barbara lovingly, "we haven't looked at the Log for ages."

Looking around, she continued, "say, is it okay for everyone in the room to be here? Maybe together we can come up with ideas to help the others."

"Sure—of course. We're all in this together."

"Day one—Vienna."

"Vienna?" asked Mary, fingering her broad-rimmed hat. "There was a Whereever in Vienna?"

"Dear," explained Penny, Mary's housemate and co-Mother, "if we comment on every entry in that thick Journal, we'll never hear it all." Then she returned to folding the hem of her apron.

"I'm afraid Penny's right—you see, I wrote everything down in as much detail as possible."

"I'll be quiet," said Mary—"but *Vienna?*"

"What a grand place—if that's where we really are. No wonder so many musicians have lived and flourished here."

"Dear ..." interrupted Barbara. "You see ... uh ... I've read your Journal about the Tour already. When he returned from the Grand Tour, Larry was upset and didn't like the idea one bit of you putting all the details in black and white. I think he said it's 'too concrete' and 'too permanent'. Anyway, Larry convinced me to show him where you kept your Journal," Barbara confessed.

"Oh dear, *I'm so sorry,"* she said with a sigh.

"No harm done, Barb. Who knows, maybe it helped break up the Experiment. Anyway, shall I continue?"

"Of course—I just wanted to say that the reason I said this was to ... well...."

"What dear? I don't think I wrote anything personal here—did I?"

"No you didn't, Johnny. But you did say a lot that's not germane at the moment. Maybe you could skip through all the descriptive parts and just mention names."

"Names?"

"Yes, the names of the residents at all those places. That's what we're most interested in, isn't it—so we can contact them?"

"I suppose so. Okay, let me glance through.... The problem is that I didn't emphasize *residents,* because I was more interested in Recruiters and the mood of each place. But here we go."

"Check the margins," suggested Barbara. "I recall scribbles in the margins."

"You have a keen eye, my love. But I don't see how we can possibly contact all the other Whereever residents with only their names."

Skipping and scanning, I leafed through the now-famous Leprechaun Log.

"Ah here," I said. "In Vienna, there's Malcolm McLaren, James Donnel, Hans Struber, Ricardo Hermanes. Say, there's more here than I thought—I must've been in quite a daze throughout the Tour. Anyway, at the bottom of the page there's also the name Ricardo followed by Zaragoza."

"Is that a person or a town?" asked Barbara.

"Town," replied Ben Bow—"it's in the north of Spain."

"Well, it's a lead, anyway. But I wonder how many Ricardos there are in Zaragoza. Where's the next one, Johnny?" asked Barbara.

"Before I take you to Nepal, the Viennese Recruiter was named Bascomb."

"Bully!" said Glenn Mye rhymes-with-eye impatiently. "On to Nepal, Johnny—who was the Recruiter there?"

"Lung Chu. It was quiet there...."

I skimmed just enough to give my friends a taste of the Tour, instead of only a roll call. "Prayer wheels ... the Shops.... Oh yeah, I remember. The Viennese Shops seemed alive with music and dancing, and Bascomb wore those stylish Austrian shorts. But in Nepal, each Shop was like one big meditation. Somewhere here.... Yes, Lung Chu is my notion of a Guru or Zen Master."

"Johnny, that's great," said Stan Lew. "But what about the names of other apprentices—our Asian counterparts? Time's a-wasting, and we do have to go to work tomorrow...."

"Right ..."

"Well, here's Omar Turu—I think he was from Turkey. Kim Suan, Vivek Gupta, Oso Isaki.... Aha, here's what looks like a town by the name of Ulaanbaanter. Well, if Sherlock Holmes is in the crowd, we know who to contact for help."

"How many places are there, Johnny? You've mentioned a center for Europe, and now Asia—was there one for every continent?"

"Yes, plus the Arctic and Antarctic. Let's see … the next stop was Africa. Pauul was the Recruiter and the village was in the Congo—everyone was black.… Yes, I wrote something on how Native Africans *act* compared to Afro-Americans. Seems.…"

"I'm sure that's interesting, Johnny. But we're after names, remember?"

"Well," I replied, forcing myself away from the entries—"I can't decipher my own writing. The Congo sounds were so unfamiliar and phonetics didn't make it any easier. But there are still a lot of Oomba-Oombo's and Unga-Ungo's. Oh, here's the only one that makes sense to me—Daniel Ookama from Johannesburg."

"Bravo, Johnny! You wouldn't think there'd be too many Daniel Ookama's in the Johannesburg phone directory, would you? Maybe we can contact him and ask for the names of others in his group. What's next?"

"Don't rush me. Here's Daniel—he was incredible. I almost felt he could have been a soul mate. Can people of the same gender and Race be soul mates without …?"

"I don't know," replied Mike McGee. "Maybe if you go find the guy, you'll figure it out. But keep going, will you?"

"Well, there you have the Congo Whereever, ladies and gentlemen."

"Okay, on to Uberlandia, South America. Let's see … Julio the Recruiter … confusing … hyped beings … old attuned souls … liveliness and sobriety.…"

"Names, did you include *names?*"

"Well, here are some chicken tracks that might be Paulo, Alexandro, Juan Marconi … how about Pedro Alverez? Oh, I remember him—big fella.…"

"Any towns, Johnny—anywhere we could search?"

"Yes, Brasilia. But finding anyone there would be like finding a needle in a haystack. I imagine there are oodles of Marconis and Alverezes in Brasilia."

"Well," remarked Mike, "it's a starting place. Where'd you and Larry go next, Johnny?"

"By the way," interjected Ben. "How did you and our Recruiter from North America hold up during the Tour?"

"No sweat—we had endless energy. Of course, I must've been hypnotized, and Larry took a break once."

"Maybe we can show-and-tell the personal stuff later, dear," said Barbara quickly. "Who's next?"

"Recruiter Sidge at the North Pole."

"You're kidding."

"I swear by an igloo. But, Sidge.… Yes, here he is … zillions of people.… Are they all Leprechauns? Innocent … simple.… Could stay there forever if I wouldn't freeze."

"Did you get any names, Johnny?"

"How about Oonga, Poliinka, Myrtwp—man, these are wild. Even if I had a full name and address, I don't know how we could track anyone down. You know, they're nomads—

moving from place to place. But come to think of it, the South Pole was even worse."

"My," said Sally McGee, "the Experiment was more extensive than we ever could've imagined. I thought we were the only people, yet there seem to be hordes of others located all over the world. I have a feeling it was good that you Grumpys busted the whole thing apart before the Leprechauns did any real damage."

"That," said Glenn, "is exactly why Ben, Stan, and I left. But it wasn't until Johnny joined us that we realized *something* had to be done—and quickly. Yes, the Leprechauns had a strong plan, and they were executing it well."

"You know, Barbara," said Stan, "though maybe you don't. But the bottom-line reason we thought of capturing Larry and doing what we did was because of you."

"Me …? How is that—what did I have to do with your revolution? I was sitting quietly in Whereever when everything happened."

"What did you have to do with it all?" Stan replied with a chuckle. "Everything, that's all. It was because Johnny couldn't stand being away from you while you were under Larry's thumb—or whatever. Your hubby almost died thinking he might never see you again."

"Is that true, Johnny?" asked Barbara, sliding her arm around my shoulder. "Did you miss your dear, sweet Barb?"

"Believe it, dear. But right now, I'm on a roll—and almost finished. You can show me how grateful you are when we're alone."

"Bravo!" said Mike, "so what's left on Magellan's itinerary?"

"Only one more—Brian and the Australian Outback."

"Brian," said Ben Bow. "I remember him—Larry called him the King."

"And deservedly. Brian was *the* Recruiter, as in Super-Recruiter."

"Good," said Mike, "and who did he recruit—did you get any names at his Whereever?"

But I became engrossed in the Journal again, and read silently.

"Yo, Johnny-boy! *Names?*"

"Can't help it—this Brian really is something. My guess is that wherever he is doing whatever he does, he will make a difference. He's a born leader—and more than that, he's an initiator, a follow through-er, and a closer. Amazing how this Lep seems like he could pull anything off."

"Names?"

"Okay. So, let's see.… My first note is to ask Larry how this Leprechaun, who looks and acts like an Aborigine, is named Brian. Hmmm … the people at his place were definitely not one hundred-percent Aborigine.…"

"Interesting, but.…"

"… Bone in his nose … Prize Recruiter.…"

"Too bad we don't have him here instead of the Journal," said Glenn. "We could shake the names of the apprentices out of him."

"… Imp … dancing … diamond-brilliant eyes.…"

"I'm glad you fell in love with the guy, Johnny. But did you get any names?"

"Say, here's a summary of the Grand Tour," I said, ignoring everyone.

"Wish I could hear it," said Penny, "but I have to take the kids home."

"It's short. *The Tour was an amazing success. Not all Leprechauns are the same. Can a hybrid Lep like me visit other Whereevers at will, or was this a special trip? Why did Larry take me on the Grand Tour anyway? Why didn't Barb come along? And in a side note, Larry said Leps don't need to communicate by out-and-out words—everything happens by osmosis.*"

"Should have used *telepathically*," I added pensively. "Anyway, in that case, I hope everything sinks in soon. How's that, gang?"

"Bravo," said Glenn, "excellent reporting. I take it there are no more names in the margin of your Pulitzer Prize winning work."

"Not one."

"Bummer," remarked Stan.

"Not really," countered Glenn. "You see, while Johnny was reading—or perhaps musing—I was thinking. It occurred to me that there's more than one way to *trick a Leprechaun,* so to speak. In other words, why not contact all the recruits simultaneously, instead of one by one?"

"Like get on the Leprechaun hot line—and learn how to broadcast an invitation telepathically? Maybe recapture Larry, and force him to be our *Spokes-Imp?*"

"I'm serious—we put ads in the major newspapers of each region. Each one says something like, 'If you're a survivor of the Experiment and want to contact others, please write to such and such address,' or something like that. In this way, we can reach many people without having to travel around the world or run up a million-dollar phone bill."

"Now we're getting somewhere!" said Stan.

I might have added something more, but my nose was still in the Journal.

The only thing that pulled it out was Barbara, whispering softly, "So you missed me, did you, *Mr Committed?*"

CHAPTER 43

▼

Larry was keen to visit Here and Now. Once he arrived, however, he had second thoughts. "Oh they look so happy, don't they now? Aye, their Shops, sweet children, and marital bliss—'tis just like Whereever. But we'll not forget what they are, because no matter how ideal things look, they are Human to the core—and everyone knows what that means...."

The Leprechaun remained skeptical and cautious as he hovered invisibly above the housing development in a form no Man could have detected.

"Calm down, Larry dear," soothed Lucy.

But Larry wouldn't, or couldn't—"Oh, if I could just get my hands on that Johnny McMann, I'd settle everything!"

"Now, now, dear," implored Lucy. "You're just carrying on this way because of the way he treated you. The word in the hedge ... you know, from Jenny, Sean and Sarah—Leprechauns you love and trust—the word is that Johnny and the whole lot of Humans want to make amends for what they did."

Larry was about to break into another fit, when Lucy continued, "besides, dear, the feeling is that Johnny was forced to do what he did—otherwise, he would never have gotten his beloved Committed back. Forced, do you hear darling—*forced.*"

"Forced, borscht!" said Larry, barely hearing her. "A *fair weather friend* if ever there was one. One day a-traipsing around the world, talking to every Leprechaun he meets as if he's one himself. And the next, jumping on me, manhandling me, and cutting m'very beard off! And ... and with a dull clam shell, too! *I tell ya'....* "

Nothing could calm the Leprechaun down, though he hadn't lost his temper for eons. That is to say, he hadn't lost his temper since the last invasion by the Giants. But Lucy knew, as well as any Leprechaun, that Larry's sweet nature would return once his beard grew back.

"Oh, you'll be as sprightly as in days of old when your beloved beard grows out—for sure," said Lucy. Out loud, she added thoughtfully, "if only that Bubbo hadn't come *grumping* around wanting his revenge on all Humans in the world!"

The very mention of the word 'grump,' even though aimed at Bubbo, set Larry off again. "Why, that no-good, worthless, pea-brained Johnny...."

After the two were back at John-O'-Groats, and Larry was sufficiently holed up in his favorite briar patch, Lucy reported to Brian. "Sleeping like a baby, he is. Now we just let him cool off—then remind him of his promise. Everything should happen according to our plan."

"You got him to make a promise?" asked Brian.

"Not really," admitted Lucy. "You see, when the sweet dear is in one of his moods, he doesn't remember well. So when he comes out of the briars, I'll simply tell him what I want—as if I'm reminding him about what he promised, don't you see? He's not the Leprechaun he used to be, since being captured and humiliated."

"Whatever it takes—and I really mean that. I sense that the future of our Race depends on Larry getting his happiness back. 'Tis bad enough that we have Bubbo to answer for. But Larry—oh, I sincerely hope he will recover, lest he lose his *twinkle* for all eternity."

Brian paused, then inquired absently, "and what promise will you remind Larry that he made, Lucy dear?"

"Oh, you know—to visit Here and Now *in body,* instead of only in his mind, as he just did. The lad's so good at imagining things that he can convince himself he's actually done this or that, just because he's imagined the likes."

"And you said I was the tricky one, you did," mused Brian triumphantly. "In any case, when your Committed comes up for fresh air, would you also remind him that he promised to take me along with him when he tours this Human Village? I'd like to see his reactions first-hand, I would."

When Larry peeked from behind the thorn bushes, Lucy encouragingly announced, "Here's Brian, dear. All ready to go with you."

"And where would that be to, love?"

"To fulfill your promise, of course. 'Twill be a bad day in Leprechaun Land when one of our own makes a promise to the King and doesn't keep it, won't it now?"

CHAPTER 44

▼

Every Here and Now-er was there—at the surprise baby shower for Barbara that I had organized. Tammy, Barbara's friend and Maid of Honor, was invited; as well as Sheila, my secretary; and Barry and Pam Clarke, for whom I had located an ideal home. Mary was held up dressing two children—and with Mary-Penny-Midge's joint children, the party was certainly going to be lively.

Everyone laughed and joked as deliciously pungent aromas swirled from the grills. The baby shower went well, with the Mother-to-be enjoying every moment. Mary and Nancy were unofficial hostesses, since they were already Mothers. Because they were so busy chatting and reminiscing with Midge while holding each other's children, they often neglected their duties—but no one minded. The entire shower was just one more pleasant reason to be together and celebrate.

As the festivities progressed, Jenny Oliver and the two Lowreys had vague fears that Midge would expose them as true Leprechauns—or Jenny did anyway. Especially since Larry had let her coach the apprentices on how to become invisible.... So if Midge just added two and two together, Jenny would be exposed. Luckily, Midge always seemed preoccupied with the playful horde of children.

As the joyful baby shower continued, Larry and Brian hovered overhead. They actually hovered everywhere because their molecules were so spread-out—and continued watching in their dispersed and undetected *spirit* forms.

If they had localized and been in either Leprechaun or Human form while still invisible, one of the Humans might have sensed their presence—that's how effective the training at Whereever had been. Though they did not know it, the Whereever residents at the shower had nearly become Leprechauns during their apprenticeship in Whereever.

Jenny and the Lowreys, on the other hand, were Extraordinary Leprechauns—and could make themselves dense enough to pass as Humans. They knew what was happening and had, in fact, helped set up the party so their Leprechaun visitors would see the Here and Now Community at its finest. Jenny, the most extroverted of the moles, was about to begin gently re-directing the shower-talk when Barry Clarke beat her to it.

"Say, Johnny, whatever happened to that fellow I met in your office some time back? The tall fellow dressed in tweed—even wore brogues and a tam, if I'm not mistaken. He seemed awfully Scottish with his orange beard and all."

"Oh, Larry. He holed up somewhere...."

"Yes, Larry Lepricorn. I remember now, because his name sounded like 'Leprechaun', and it made me wonder if a Wee One could reach the size of a Man. If so, I thought he'd probably look like your friend."

Hearing everything, Larry nudged Brian—"did ya' hear that, Yer Majesty? Why, the Man's a liar as well as a beard-shaver!"

"What do you mean, a liar? Johnny said the truth as far as I know it—you did bury yourself in your thorn-patch, didn't you?" declared Brian.

"'Aye, but *holed up* 'tisn't the same as closing the doors of yer house and not wanting visitors, and ya' know it. The Human hasn't changed a bit!"

"Calm down," advised Brian, "or you'll become so dense you'll materialize. And then, won't you be in a fix?"

"Maybe that'd be the best thing under the circumstances. That Johnny is besmirching m'very name, sir."

"Not a bit of it," soothed Brian's molecules, "they're all talking about the fellow Lepricorn, not you."

"Don't try to golden-tongue it, Brian-my-King. Johnny's black-at-heart no matter how ya' whitewash his words."

The Humans continued their conversation.

"Larry—yes, I met him once," Jenny said. "Fine fellow I thought, though a bit … uh, *sneaky*. Too bad he doesn't *pop* in again. 'Twould be nice to see how he's doing, don't you think?"

And before anyone could divert the conversation, Sarah Lowrey chimed in. "All I know is that if Larry's in hearing range, he can be assured he's welcome to visit Here and Now. Isn't that right, everyone?"

"What a darrrrling jumper!" Barbara blurted, seeing that her shower was no longer the focus of attention. "Thank you so

much, Midge—oh, when will our little one be big enough to wear it?"

Larry nudged more molecules—"What a study in Human ways. Look how they're all saying one thing, but meaning another. Everyone who's been at Whereever is trying to keep the three visitors from learning the truth—and I thought we were sneaky!"

"Whatever," shrugged Brian, "but they do seem well disposed toward you."

"Well disposed, my *arse*," growled Larry, "there're sweet-talking because of the guests."

"Well then," answered Brian, "why don't we get the guests to leave—then the apprentices can speak honestly."

"You'd lower yerself to trickery?"

"I am the King of Trickery, Larry—though I usually don't show my hand. Indeed, it would take a serious cause for me to...." But he stopped before he revealed too much. "We came here to size up the Humans' true nature, my friend. And their present capacity for making amends. If they only *act* polite, then this is not a fair test—which means that we'll have to come back again and again. And just between you and me, I'd rather finish this off right now, if possible. What do you say we turn sneaky?"

"I say *no*," insisted Larry firmly. "I wasn't keen on this visit in the first place. As to trickery, never—I've pulled my last prank with those scoundrels. On the other hand, if I n*ever* come back here, 'twill be too soon. *Then again...."*

"In other words, it's up to me." Brian immediately communicated telepathically with Jenny Oliver, *'tis time to do your magic, Jenny dear—you know what I mean.'*

Jenny perked up like only a Leprechaun can—she smiled, her eyes *twinkled,* and she beamed.

Before anyone could say *SeanSeamus-JohnO'Groats-Mac Gillicuddy,* all who had not visited Whereever were headed out the door and on their way.

Brian stated majestically, "And *that's* why Jenny Oliver is here."

With Tammy, Sheila, and the Clarkes gone, everyone felt uninhibited. The group opened up just as Brian had expected, and began chatting about Larry and Whereever.

During the discussion that followed, Larry was quiet enough to hear them say things like, "We've been trying to communicate with him," "Doesn't he know we never meant him any harm?" "Why doesn't he answer?" and "I hope we haven't scared him off forever."

Brian whispered, "Lucy tells me that you have very delicate feelings, Larry. After what you've been through, I understand how difficult it must be to show them, to be sure. But please try not to be too sensitive."

After taking all of this in, Larry's wounds finally began to heal—to the point that he considered materializing at that very moment.

"Not yet," cautioned Brian. "Timing is vital—and they might be saying those things because it's a party."

Larry nodded in agreement, though he secretly wanted to join the group and apologize.

"Aye," said the King, "we'll see what our moles think of all this before doing anything more."

CHAPTER 45

▼

For untold years, Larry had been the epitome of Leprechaun gaiety, but humiliatingly beardless, he was still the most unhappy one in all Leprechaundom. While the second honeymoon with Lucy, and reconnaissance trip with Brian, had lifted his *spirits*—in time, he fell back into melancholy at home. His mood was up one day and down the next—making him feel like a yo-yo on a string. He was so moody that he himself wasn't sure what was coming next.

"Perk up, my love," encouraged Lucy. "Brian says 'twas a good trip, and you saw Sean and Sarah, dull as they sometimes are—and pretty Jenny too. Isn't she just as pretty as a flower in the early morning sunshine? And what about plump Midge, who's nearly a Leprechaun in her own right—and all due to your excellent training? Brian told me that you were about to say 'how-dee-doo' to the lot of them and make amends then and there."

"Lucy, lass, I didn't understand a single word ya' said after *'Perk'*. Sounded like a lot of gushing and roaring by a waterfall, it did." The former Recruiter chuckled silently—*'Ah, the lass means well, and I do love her dearly.'*

So the reconciliation between Human and Leprechaun— that is, between Larry and Johnny—waxed and waned according to their moods. But, all in all, it seemed like only a matter of time until everything would return to normal.

That is, until a minor catastrophe occurred.

One day, Sean Lowrey sent a *red alert*.

"My gracious!" shrieked Lucy, after receiving the message—and she wasn't a shrieker by nature.

"*What's wrong*, Lucy dear?" demanded Larry.

"The Lowreys say that Johnny's gone berserk, and you know they're not prone to exaggeration. It seems that Johnny's all bent out of shape, since he became convinced that Midge is a Leprechaun spy."

"Now what would give him that idea? Certainly she's highly developed—everyone knows that—but…."

"But what, Larry?" she replied.

"Well," replied Larry, "I should think any Human would feel proud and downright *honored* to be mistaken for a Leprechaun—*Aye.*"

"Well said," remarked Brian, who had also received the message. "The problem is that Johnny feels Leprechaun trickery is scandalous. He's taken this as heatedly as you, Larry, have taken being shaved."

"But *Midge*," emphasized Lucy, "she's such a dear, even though she isn't a true Leprechaun. I should think that

Johnny would be more concerned about the real thing—you know, Sean, Sarah, and Jenny."

"He would if he knew they were Leprechauns," explained Brian. "At any rate, one day Johnny saw Midge sitting with those six children, having a good time as Midge always does. But the lass was only half-visible. Sean says Johnny just exploded, so mad he was."

"Partially visible, ya' say?" said Larry, smiling. "Well then, 'tis proof that not all Humans are completely dense!"

"Aye, Larry," Brian agreed. "'Tis proof you recruited and trained well. But Johnny *is* in a rage—and we know what that could lead to amongst Humans."

Larry instinctively grabbed the stubble on his chin. "Yes—he might vent his rage on us the way his ancestors did in the past, and the way his Grumpys did to me—Beware!"

"Could be a holocaust," added Brian. "Not just a minor vendetta against you or me, or any other Recruiter. This could lead to out-and-out war, and doesn't bode well for any of us."

Now it was Larry's turn to blow his cork. *"Blast it all!"* roared the little fellow, "'Tis nothing but the temperamental quirk of the bloody Human Race. I tell ya', Brian, not a one of them is trustworthy. And this Johnny McMann's at the top of the list. Furthermore...."

"Oh ... Larry," admonished Lucy.

"Just think of the glen and heather, and your sweet briar patch," said Brian smoothly and in his most diplomatic voice. Naturally, he erased 'Man', 'Human', 'People', and definitely 'Johnny' from his vocabulary for the moment. While the embers of the Johnny-Larry feud smoldered, Brian knew this recent outbreak could spread like wildfire against all Leprechauns if not handled delicately.

Lucy picked up on Brian's tactic. "Larry dear, do you remember how grand and glorious our vacation was? Here, there, and everywhere we went—seeing the sights most Leprechauns dream about, but seldom ever see. What a warmth in the heart it spread, my Larry. Oh my Committed, we could enjoy that wonderful bliss again … and forever."

"Aye," said Brian, keeping the diversion alive, "and after that, perhaps a trip to Leprechaun Land—haven't been there for ages myself." He almost added, 'since the Experiment,' but realized that might send his friend into a new set of paroxysms.

But Larry wasn't up to a vacation, or even the Leprechaun's most sacred place—his rollercoaster emotions couldn't have withstood either. Instead, the Wee Imp moved deep into a very thorny and isolated hedge in his wrinkled tweeds. He brooded, pouted, moped, and fretted—and when the lad was in that condition, well, it was best to leave him alone. That is, unless he did something drastic.

Since he retreated moodily to his thorny hedge instead of calling all Leprechauns, Elementals and Forces Above to take arms and haunt Humans 'til the end of eternity, Lucy and Brian left him alone … which was, in fact, quite propitious.

CHAPTER 46

▼

Like Larry Leprechaun, I was also known for my sound reasoning and admirable stability—unless I felt someone was trying to hoodwink me. But having been tricked once, it was most unlikely that it would ever happen to me again—unless, of course, the perpetrator had *exceptional* hoodwinking talent. So, when Midge appeared half-vanished, I reverted to what the Leprechauns called *brute* or *beast*—or some such *b*-word that they hated to give voice to, being as delicate as they are.

I was in a rage.

Barging into Midge's room, I yelled, *"You're a Leprechaun!"* The six children, not accustomed to such outbreaks, hid behind the gentle Mother. "You're a spy, and you're trying to convert us. Why, I'll have none of this at Here and Now … especially with my wife pregnant—what's your plan, you traitor, to snatch our child the day it's born?"

Mary instinctively grabbed her hat, Nancy clutched her apron, and both protected their friend and six children. They'd never seen me speak so vehemently, and they weren't going to take any chances.

"I swear on my Mother's heart that I'm Human just like you," pleaded Midge. "Sure, they worked on me at Whereever—I was the first there. They schooled me, and trained me the best they could. And yes, they nearly had me—but Johnny, I swear I'm Human just like you!"

"Oh?" I snapped back, puffing in self-righteousness, "then why can't *I* disappear—or anyone else here, for that matter? *Tell me that, Midge Leprechaun!"*

"I don't know … maybe it's because I'm so sensitive, so … susceptible. The Leprechauns commented about it, and gave me extra attention to develop the skill.…"

"Johnny, *please,*" intervened Jenny, hurrying into the room when she heard the commotion. "Midge is such a dear—and I'm sure she's telling the truth."

"Thank you, Jenny," said Midge, "you're a dear, yourself. When I first got there, you.…"

"First got there? *Got where—Whereever?* This means that you, Jenny Oliver, are also a Leprechaun!"

The Lowreys, listening in the hallway, became duller than dull.

"Out!" I demanded.

"Please, dear," Barbara soothed, though she needed more soothing than anyone since her unborn baby was becoming more and more lively. "Midge.…"

"Midge—*smidge!*" I bellowed.

"You should know, Midge Knight, that I'll have no Leprechauns in my development—*Out, I say!* And tell your Leprechaun friends that we've had our fill of tricks and

Experiments, lies and treachery. I'll shave every two-faced Imp I get my hands on."

"And you leave too, Jenny Oliver—you're obviously one of them too!" I spat, obviously out of control.

It's not that half of the residents at Here and Now lined up on one side of the Community Center, with the other half facing them—but there was a definite difference of opinion in the room. And since Johnny, the usual calm arbiter, was incapable of playing that role, Mike McGee took over.

"Hey everyone, just *calm down*." With that, Sally stood close enough to reinforce her husband's diplomatic stance.

"Now, Johnny, I'm not going to criticize you for feeling the way you do, as that would only perpetuate ill feelings. But I do want you to know that Midge is no Leprechaun—I know. Remember, I'm the *original spy*, and Midge is just what she claims to be—sensitive, and susceptible to training and the power of suggestion. But she's definitely *not* a Leprechaun."

Glenn Mye rhymes-with-eye jumped on the bandwagon. "Incidentally—as I recall, the Here and Now bylaws state that no individual owns the development. This means that no one has the power to toss anyone else out, right? The whole idea behind the addition was that it was a group endeavor. And our purpose was to be a harmonious and happy community."

Sean Lowrey added solemnly, "By the way, in Jenny's defense, everyone should know that when the first apprentices arrived at Whereever, several people were already there, in addition to Jenny. So she can't be a Leprechaun either."

"That's right," said Mike. "Sally and I were there. Ben, Stan …" he continued. Mentioning the Grumpys, whom Johnny respected highly, was enough.

"All right! *All right!* Then please explain why I saw, clear as day and with my own two eyes, Midge *half-vanished.*"

"Habit," said the accused softly. "The Leprechauns knew how innocent I was, so they trained me and worked on me until their techniques worked as naturally and effectively as breathing."

"Oh, that's fine and *dandy.*"

Sensing an advantage, I continued with the questioning, "that was while you were *there*—but you're *here* now. So why are you still using their techniques, unless you are a Leprechaun?"

Midge looked down at the floor. Her tranquil nature wouldn't allow her to stand against opposition, and all she could do was mutter softly, "out of habit."

To which Jenny quickly added, "and just because we were all at Whereever, that doesn't mean we're *all* Leprechauns— *does it, Johnny?*"

Holding her belly, Barbara spoke lovingly, "Midge dear, I feel we've known each other for a long time, even before the Experiment. You're such a *sweetie,* and I want you and your darling children to stay. Now, if we're taking a vote, let my 'yea' be officially recorded."

"Oh Barb, that's not necessary," whispered Midge with relief.

"Good," said Mike. "It is neither necessary nor desirable to attack anyone here. Remember, this is a place of harmony.

Still, I think it would be good to remind ourselves of the ground rules, so we can live together happily."

"Okay … uhh … I'm sorry about the confusion—all this Leprechaun trickery has been so trying. Uhh … my apologies to you all," I reluctantly confessed. "As far as the rules—yes … none of us interferes in any other resident's life, no matter how much they'd like to. And everyone is free to be themselves," I stated humbly.

"Well said, Johnny," agreed Stan, adding, "and we should also put our pasts behind us—all of us. Who cares who's done this or that? If some of us were more thoroughly trained than others, so be it. They'll just have to work on being in the present a little harder."

"But we leave Leprechaun trickery to the Leprechauns," I insisted.

"Very good," concluded Mike.

Midge sighed deeply, happy the trial was over.

CHAPTER 47

▼

One fine day, when tempers, grudges and suspicions were quiet, Brian looked toward the blue sky and said calmly, "seems like time to visit Leprechaun Land."

The statement hit Larry like a ton of bricks.

"You've been there, have ya', Brian?"

"I have—and twice, to be exact."

As soon as Brian spoke, Larry lost all thought of everything else. His mind focused on the land sacred to Leprechauns—a trip there would be the pinnacle experience of a Leprechaun's life.

"I'd like to go with ya'," Larry said flatly.

"I'm sure you would," said Brian, with a faraway look—he was already beginning to feel the transformation necessary to visit the Great Land. "The truth is that you can go only when you're *capable* of going. It's the same thing we told the apprentices about becoming Leprechauns—*either you're ready, or you're not.*"

"But Brian, I've a red hot itch to go."

"That's the worst sign, Larry. 'Tis first cousin to holding onto the un-Leprechaun-like grudge against Johnny McMann and Humans." Though Brian was as diplomatic as possible, he knew he was facing a hot-tempered Larry.

Larry's flash of anger didn't develop. He finally realized that no matter how badly he wanted to go to the place held Holy by all Leprechauns, he simply couldn't. And so, slowly—though more like a pleasant fade-out than vanishing—Brian disappeared, leaving Larry standing alone.

If a movie director were filming this scene, he would find it impossible to capture that land where Brian the King went, since it was purely abstract. Not a place—no rule by entities of any kind, and beyond time and space. There would be nothing at all to film—the closest the director could get might be wisps of pastel colors, and silent, pleasant sounds. Perhaps the highly creative Man might dare to show pure black, and cover it with a soft narrative of what he thinks Leprechaun Heaven is like.

And, because this 'Land' is a state of non-being where time doesn't exist, it's only possible to estimate or approximate how long Brian spent in that divine state. Perhaps three hundred Leprechaun years ... but, it could have also been thirty seconds or three eons. It really didn't matter, because states like this can't be marked or measured by time. However long it was, when the highly developed Leprechaun opened his *twinkling* eyes, he faced the menacing figure of Bubbo-the-Outcast, the original Leprechaun Grumpy.

"So," snarled Bubbo, "the *King's* been sneakin' off to the Holy Land, have ya' now?"

"Ah, how nice of you to greet me upon my return, Bubbo," said Brian happily, "though you know well I haven't been anywhere."

"Indeed. Been there myself, if ya' recall."

Because Larry was sitting in the thorn patch from which Brian had faded, he saw and heard the two quite easily. He stared in amazement—'*How could Bubbo, of all Leprechauns, have been to Leprechaun Land? It's Holy. Yet, as certain as ya' say 'ouch' when poked by a thistle, that bitter outcast has indeed been there!*'

"Well, *Mista* Brian," snorted Bubbo. "Hope ya' enjoyed that *last* visit to Faerie Land."

"Last you say, my friend?" said Brian, who was completely at ease—as they all are when they return.

"Aye. Decided, I have, that since I can't *dilute* the brutish nature of Man by changing 'em to resemble Leprechauns, I'll just destroy the magic of Leprechauns instead. An' what a better place to begin than our Holy *non-place* known as Leprechaun Land?"

"Where else?" said Brian calmly. "And since you've thought this out so well, do you know that by destroying the connection to our Sacred Place—which is itself indestructible—you may also end up destroying yourself and all Leprechauns, as well?"

"Ha!" said Bubbo, viciously. "I'm no fool. Ye' see, Brian, 'tis brutishness *and all that tolerates or supports it* that must be eliminated completely—collateral damage is an accepted fact these days."

After having experienced the Ultimate State that all Leprechauns seek, how could Bubbo be so destructive? Legend has it that it began eons before, when Brian, Bubbo, and a few others had reappeared from the Holy Land, everyone proclaimed that Brian had the *twinkliest* eyes of all.

But Bubbo's ego couldn't stand that—he felt insulted, and it burned inside him … and in time, he turned sour. It festered through the millennia, until he had to do something or self-destruct.

Now that his Experiment had failed, Bubbo was forced to aim his venom elsewhere, and he concluded, 'where better than at *all* Leprechauns'. In his warped mind, he'd reasoned, *'I will get my revenge—and what do I have to lose? If I'm going to be ostracized for hurting one Leprechaun, why not just take their very Leprechaun essence from them all? Then I alone will be the Sovereign of Leprechaun Land!'*

"Well, Bubbo," said Brian. "'Tis a fair eye that *twinkles*. So, how…."

"Oh that's the greatness of *my* Project," said Bubbo, reeking of black bile. "And since you're so curious, I'll begin with you."

Full of himself and his Leprechaun Powers, *Bubbo then stole the very twinkle from Brian.*

"'Tis as simple as that, *Mista* Brian," laughed the evil Imp, maliciously. "And now, I simply go from one Leprechaun to the next 'til I've stolen all *twinkles,* and thereby Leprechaun Land itself. 'Tis all so simple, and well begun …!"

Larry soundlessly flattened himself against the ground, became invisible, spread his molecules out ever so thinly, and hid behind his thorn bush.

His mind raced, *'Ahh, the tale of two twinkles! The one every Leprechaun possesses, that glorious sparkle that separates them from all other creatures on earth. And then the twinkle—the Holy Twinkle—the brilliance only those who have experienced the Divine Leprechaun Land possess.'* Larry, of course, had the *twinkle,* but not the Holy *Twinkle.* Even without it, he knew he had to do something to save the essence of his King and fellow Elementals.

"There, *Majesty,*" said Bubbo, triumphantly. "With one fell swoop, I've achieved more than the entire foolish Experiment. Now you can never return to Leprechaun Holy Land! And soon, I'll neutralize the power every Imp possesses, since they'll be taken by surprise," he cackled.

"No one even suspects a thing—farewell, low-life!"

Very quietly, Larry's alert mind began to plan, *'How to pass the word so the Leprechauns won't be taken by surprise? Oh, Land of all that's Holy, it's up to me!'*

CHAPTER 48

▼

Larry didn't know every Leprechaun who had been to Leprechaun Land. He didn't need to, of course, since he could contact them telepathically *en masse*. But he had enough presence of mind to know that the instant he sent a *red alert*, Bubbo would mute him.

At the same time, he was also aware that the Lowreys and Jenny Oliver had all but tuned out of the psychic hotline, for fear their identities would be compromised. So Larry, no slouch of a Leprechaun, yet not in the same league as Bubbo, did the only thing he could think of—he went to Here and Now *in person* to inform them.

Before he left, Lucy asked, "Why are Brian and the others so quiet—is that what happens when you visit the Holy Land?"

Larry was too anxious to explain, being caught up in his urgent thoughts—*'I must get to Here and Now right instantly! I must alert them before Bubbo gets there—even if it means falling into Johnny's hands again!'*

Although it was with some apprehension, Larry whisked himself off to the Humans' housing development—the very place he'd hoped to never visit again. He was only partially aware that if Bubbo figured out what he was up to, Larry would only be the first casualty. Bubbo would certainly also steal Sean, Sarah, and Jenny's *twinkles*—and then the great Grumpy would mute all the other Leprechauns *forever*.

Hovering invisibly outside the Community Center, Larry surveyed the area. As desperate as he was, he didn't dare enter immediately—especially since the very person he least wanted to see was the only one visible outside. *'But I have to contact an Exalted One now!'*

Swallowing his pride, Larry said aloud, "Johnny—Johnny McMann. I've an urgent message to deliver." He remained invisible.

Recognizing the voice of my former friend and Recruiter, I replied, "*Well,* if it isn't Larry Lepricorn himself. I thought—and hoped—I'd seen the last of you."

"*Yes, yes,*" answered Larry hastily, "but that's not what's important at the moment."

"And what *is* important, you rogue?"

"A message of the gravest importance—that's what. And quit dilly-dallying around, or it'll be too late."

"Well, if it's so important and time-sensitive, then why don't you just deliver it *yourself?*"

"Because...." Larry's mind raced, *'Blast it Man, you're eating up precious time!'*

"Johnny, if I don't deliver this message to … to an Exalted, it may well be the death and destruction of all Leprechauns, and Leprechaundom as well."

"You don't say!—Well now, you're in quite a predicament, aren't you?"

"I am," confessed Larry. "And irony of ironies, 'tis yerself who can solve it all. I only ask that ya' enter yer big dwelling there, and announce that Larry's outside awaiting anyone who's been to *The Land*."

"And who might that be?" I asked, finally becoming interested.

There was now real reason to make the messenger squirm—"What Leprechaun spy lives at Here and Now?"

"No matter, Man. *Just do as I ask, and quickly!*"

Just then, Bubbo *popped* into view.

Now, I'd never seen the *Darth Vader* of Leprechauns—only heard such a one existed. Luckily, my intuition worked well enough to pick up his darkness—*'this one smells of evil'*. But I just didn't know the extent of it.… For all I knew, the Imp in front of me could just as easily have been the president of the United States in disguise.

"Johnny," whispered Larry, "that's *Bubbo* … he's here to.…"

"Why, hello sir," I introduced myself with a smile. "My name's Johnny, Johnny McMann. And you—you're Bubbo, aren't you?"

Then I reached out and grabbed Bubbo's hand in greeting—"Let me shake your hand."

"Yeah, I'm Bubbo. But how'd ya'...." Before the Great Grumpy could even finish his sentence, his hand felt as if it were securely held in a tight vise.

"Glad to meet you, Bubbo—*very glad, indeed.*"

"You're squeezing my hand, sir—and 'tis really hurting. A wee bit, anyway."

"A *wee* bit—sounds like you have a bit of the Scot in you, eh?"

"Way back, aye," said Bubbo, beginning to sense that he had foolishly fallen into a trap. "No more than you, I'd say—you've a Scottish name as well. But *mista,* please let go of my hand...."

At that very moment, several former Here and Now residents exited from the center, including Jenny Oliver, Mike McGee, and both Lowreys.

"Don't look!" yelled Larry, who'd materialized behind the two who were shaking hands.

Instantly, the three Leprechauns turned.

Mike, seeing me holding onto the stranger with vigor, sized up the situation in a flash. He grabbed Bubbo's free hand, and a titanic struggle ensued. But Mike and I, who'd successfully wrestled one Leprechaun into submission, were used to such twisting and squirming. With our very dense Human bodies atop his, Bubbo couldn't do a thing but scream.

Amidst the twisting, squirming, and screaming, Larry quietly whisked the Lowreys aside.

"Stole their *twinkles*—surely the single most dastardly act a Leprechaun can perform! Infinitely worse than destroying their happiness, or even violating their Committedness." Sean replied, in his characteristic monotone.

"Aye, but he can't be allowed to steal everyone's *twinkle—that's why I've come here.*"

"*Of course,*" said Sean approvingly, now more animated than anyone at Here and Now had ever seen him.

Bubbo, that most Extraordinary and Exalted Leprechaun, suddenly used his great power in one desperate surge for freedom.

But even more quickly, I yelled, "*Ben Bow!—Stan Lew!—We have a live one here!*"

The two recognized the cry for help and leapt through the Community Center door just before Bubbo was about to free himself. Luckily, they arrived just an instant before Bubbo would have been able to escape. If they'd been even one second later, Bubbo would have vanished or de-molecularized, and then continued with his dirty duty. But Ben threw a flying tackle and grabbed the rascal's ankle—and as quick as a wink, all four of us were on the Leprechaun.

As we four pinned the intruder to the ground, the Lowreys went into action. With Bubbo immobilized and preoccupied, Sean used his Exalted Powers to take away Bubbo's own *twinkle.*

"*Ha!*" shrieked Sarah, more Leprechaun than Human—"you've stopped him!"

"Aye," said Larry anxiously. "Now we must re-light the *twinkle* in Brian and any others that Bubbo muted—oh, *how many others?*"

"Bubbo, how many did ya' de-*twinkle* before arriving at Here and Now?"

Sean stepped forward and spoke calmly, as if the worst of the battle was over. "Larry lad, you're quite knowledgeable and clever. After all, you *were* a Recruiter. But you don't know all the 'ins' and 'outs' of Exalted Leprechauns—those who've been to *The Land.* Believe me lad, part of that magic is that the instant Bubbo was de-*twinkled,* all those whom he had robbed have regained theirs."

I looked up, confident we Grumpys had secured our prisoner—who turned wet-noodle the instant his *twinkle* was gone. "This all happened so fast—I still don't know who this fellow is, and what all this *twinkle*-robbing is about. I only know it took a brave soul to come into what you must consider enemy territory, Larry. I respect you for that."

"Ye' don't need to bow to me," answered Larry, as he straightened his tam-o'-shanter. "For the single most important thing in Leprechaundom is that ya' continue to hold the initiator of The Experiment, and potential destroyer of Leprechaun Life, right where he is."

"This Bubbo fellow, then, he's the cause of all our misery— *not you, Larry?*"

"To be sure," said Sean Lowrey, authoritatively.

Enough authority that, for the first time, I stared at him. "Well, isn't this just a fine turn of events? You, Sean, and I daresay Sarah as well—you're Leprechaun spies!"

"We prefer to call ourselves *monitors,*" countered Sean. "We felt it was important to be absolutely certain where you stood regarding retaliation or revenge or … whatever."

"What horrible words," advised Sarah. "Let's just say, Johnny and you other brave fellows—that we Leprechauns are as interested as you in making amends for all the evil that's already been done."

I instinctively gave an extra twist to Bubbo's wrist.

"Which means, doesn't it, that I've been tricked again— and to make it worse, by two close friends. And irony upon irony, I'm holding and therefore solving, *your* problem. Now that's one for the books!"

Larry and the Lowreys looked humble.

Bubbo lay dazed.

"You know, I don't give a cat's whisker whether you Leprechauns go under or not. Happy one minute and manipulating the next, I really wish you'd vanish for one of your eternities. Moreover, I have half a mind to let this prisoner go. After all, I have nothing against the fellow...."

With that, I began to release my hold on Bubbo.

"*Pleeeease!*" squeaked a voice from the throng.

Everyone looked up to see who was interfering ... But Sarah instantly jumped in front of Jenny.

"Oh, *please* don't," pleaded Sarah. "We ... we'll do anything if you continue to hold the rascal."

Knowing that the Humans were also aware of the Leprechaun tendency to make and break promises as quickly as a Human can wink both eyes, Larry said, "It appears to me that two things need to be done. Because it's the most imminent, we must first deal with Bubbo. And while it's a dastardly and a most un-Leprechaun-like thing to suggest, I'm afraid the only thing to do is ... well, to do to him what Johnny did to me."

The Lowreys winced.

No one noticed Jenny following suit in the background.

"And what's the second thing, if I may ask?"

Larry lowered his head and mumbled inaudibly, "…"

"I beg your pardon, Larry," I insisted—*"I didn't hear you."*

Reluctantly, he repeated more loudly, "We're already beholden to ya' for capturing the nemesis of the Leprechauns, we are. If ya' will now shave off his badge, we'll be eternally beholden…."

"That last part, Larry—it's still a bit unclear. What was the last thing you said?

"I'll do whatever ya' ask."

CHAPTER 49

▼

Since that historic moment, Leprechauns have called Larry their greatest Hero and elevated him to Emperor status. Indeed, who but the wisest and bravest of Leprechauns could rise to the occasion and save their Exhalted King, and all other Extraordinary and Common Leprechauns? Who but the ultimate Leprechaun could be so bold, when he had nothing to gain—yet his very Leprechaunness to lose? Who but *Larry the Emperor* could be so noble as to promise a Human that he would do *anything the Human wished?* And who but the greatest and grandest would ask all Leprechauns to treat a Human like me as a Hero—for my instantaneous comprehension, and successful subduing of Bubbo?

It was a grand and glorious day of celebration—and definitely an event every Leprechaun will remember throughout eternity. Royalty was bestowed, citations were given, and medals were passed out. And the Leprechaun-Human bond that had been sought for eons was sealed. It was, indeed, a grand and glorious day.

That night, I performed a heroic act of my own when Barbara began having labor pains. After getting Barbara to the hospital, I smiled at her in joy about the upcoming birth—I was going to be a father! But, even with all the joy of the moment, *something* was nagging at me—something I couldn't quite identify. *Deep inside, some vaguely unsettling feeling lurked, much like a small pebble digging into the sole of my foot....*

Barbara gave birth to a healthy and sparkly-eyed baby boy.

Larry was at the bedside, for we had agreed to be friends again. "'Tis a fine lad ya' have there," declared the Emperor, smiling majestically. "A fine, fine lad indeed. Aye, and the truth 'tis that I'm envious—I am. 'Tisn't everyone who can be father to such a one, nor husband to such a lass!"

When we were alone, I nearly swooned when looking proudly at our little baby boy. And, it sure seemed to me that the new Mother was surrounded by a halo. I mused silently, *'my wife's an Angel for sure!'*

After the latest jubilations, no one was surprised to learn that I had agreed immediately to my wife's desire to name the little one *Lawrence*. "Seems a bit strange to name a Human child after a Leprechaun. But under the circumstances, why not? Besides—there's no law that says a Human can't have a Leprechaun for a godfather," I joked.

Promises flew left and right that day, they surely did—the former apprentices promised to never humiliate another Leprechaun; and in turn, the Leprechauns promised never to trick a Human again. Together, all vowed to love and honor each other's Race, and to come to the aid of one another when necessary. And what a grand celebration it was throughout Here and Now and all Leprechaundom.

Larry and I were again proclaimed Heroes, Bubbo had been neutralized and could cause no more mischief, Brian and his fellow Exalted Ones had their *twinkles* back, and Barbara had given birth to a beautiful baby boy—It was, indeed, a day of days.

But that little pebble kept rubbing ... yes, that irksome little ... whatever.

CHAPTER 50

▼

Never so loved was the heir to the hearts of everyone at Here and Now—baby Larry was called *Little Larry* the moment it became known that he possessed the apparatus that made him male. All women were considered 'aunts' and all men were considered 'uncles'. Teddy, Colin, Amanda, Samantha, Beebee and Deedee—the trio's children—were automatically 'brothers' and 'sisters'. The love bundle was handled and hugged by so many people that Barbara feared he might turn black and blue.

Little Larry turned out to be the perfect little *being* arriving at just the right time.

The Lowreys left Here and Now because they had to—their cover was blown when they removed Bubbo's *twinkle*. Jenny Oliver, however, slipped through the net and was not found out. When Larry called for Exalteds, everyone's attention was on the Lowreys and nobody even suspected Jenny of being a Leprechaun—let alone Extraordinary. And even though the residents felt an invisible force hovering overhead after the Lowreys departure, they attributed it to having a newborn amongst them. No one knew what it really was, nor did they attempt to identify the unusual feeling.

The word spread that in this particular housing development, everyone was happy and filled with joy. If the sparkling reputation of Here and Now had been a cake, the birth of little Larry was like the icing on the cake—and this feature gave a whole new meaning to the terms 'Ideal Village' and 'Utopia'.

Visitors marveled at the congeniality of the residents, and there was virtually no law breaking. The six children who attended Barbara's home-school elementary classes were rarely sick, and they already showed signs of being exceptional.

In the eyes of the outside world, Here and Now seemed blessed.

CHAPTER 51

▼

That blessedness was more like the calm before a storm—for there was one Silas Malddick and his band of witch hunters who were beginning to take an unhealthy interest in Here and Now.

Malddick's vigilantes didn't actually hunt witches, though they would have done so with a vengeance if he'd sensed they existed. But the group had been searching for a cause of all this joy and happiness—which they considered to be *'evil'*. According to their leader, their purpose was to exterminate any and all evil and whatever they believed to be its cause.

Silas was rotten to the core—a dropout from Sunday school, and a reject from high school and the Boy Scouts, he had run afoul of the local police on numerous occasions. His self-proclaimed mission in life was to totally ferret out and destroy *everything* that promoted joy and happiness, or smelled even faintly subjective. That included religion, spirituality, and new age *ooga-booga*.

"Only facts, do you hear? The objective, the scientific, the provable—all else falls in the *venomous pit of evil!* The subjective, intuitive, paranormal, hunches, even feelings—they're what breed superstition, and superstition breeds weakness. Weakness, in turn, brings about the corruption of Mankind. Down with Santa Claus—down with the Easter Bunny! If I find a single person who believes in Elves, Faeries, Witches or Leprechauns, I'll send the *Dogs of Hell* after them!"

If Silas wasn't menacing enough, his group known as VVV—Vigilantes against the Vile and Villainous—carried out the evil whims of their leader—like all fanatics. They acted blindly and irrationally, with no concern for innocent bystanders. The vigilante group was evil, scrawled by the psychotic and vindictive mind of its founder—and was the opposite of Here and Now.

Their leader proclaimed that nothing on earth was, or could ever be, blessed. To him, blessedness was nothing more than superstitious hogwash held by unscientific minds. As long as the residents of *any* town drank city water and breathed common air, they *must not* be happier than the rest of the nation—that would be *un*-American. So, when Silas heard that Here and Now bred only joy and happiness, he automatically became suspicious. Convinced that people aren't naturally happy, he concluded that something must be *wrong*. And once that conclusion had been drawn about Here and Now, Silas and his VVV went on the warpath. Applying his twisted methods, they first sought facts.

"Create a profile of every Man, and I suppose every Woman too, at Here and Now—and leave no stone unturned. Find every mistake that each person has ever made. Find what grades they made in what schools, who their friends were, and what organizations each has joined. And especially, any who were kicked out of or rejected by any group, and who did the kicking. Find out how they vote, if they are vegetarians, new agers, do yoga—or *anything at all unusual or suspicious.* And while you're at it, find out who goes to church, and who is homosexual."

The V's did their job zealously. They found out that my true name was Johnathan—I'd been going under a false name for years, and my income tax return was filed late the year I was elected to *Phi Beta Kappa.* Barbara skipped a class in High School Home Economics using cramps as an excuse. Mike McGee had an argument with a drunk who insisted on shaking hands with 'both of him'. Sally McGee, once Sally Traverse, had an uncle who lived in *San Francisco.* Ted Margoles switched from voting republican to democrat *for no valid reason.* Susan Margoles once modeled for a *foreign* fashion magazine. Glenn Mye rhymes-with-eye—*and it also rhymes with spy.* Ben Bow was in the Boy Scouts for nine years—but *never* reached Eagle Scout. The brother of Freeda Bow was awarded a Congressional Medal of Honor by *Jimmy Carter.* Stan Lew was *left handed.* Janice Lew once went *skinning dipping.* Teddy, Colin, Amanda, Samantha, Beebee and Deedee *never went to public school.* The baby known as Little Larry, has *never* had colic. Midge, Nancy, and Penny have *no known last names, and have been living together with Midge's husband Tory for six years. No identification has been found* for Jennifer Oliver, aka Jenny—is she an FBI Agent, does she work for the CIA, or is she under federal protection; and if so, why?

In short, they found the entire populace of Here and Now highly suspicious.

Silas Malddick's second project was to investigate friends of the suspects in question. Sheila Parker, secretary to Johnathan McMann is *Catholic*. Tammy Taylor, friend of Barbara McMann is guilty of something *by association*. Barry Clarke bought a house from the McManns, and therefore *must be up to no good*. Pam Clarke, Barry's wife, has done *nothing outstanding* in her entire life—but is Pam her real name? Lawrence Lepricorn is an odd sort of guy with an orange goatee, a tweed suit, Scottish brogue shoes, and a funny cap— *who is he, and is it all a disguise?*

Silas' conclusion: the friends of the Here and Now residents are also *highly suspicious*.

The third attempt to find the 'real dirt' on the Here and Now group came when the VVV photographed and taped everything that originated from within the development. What stood out the most was the inexplicable and often sudden appearance and absence of Jennifer Oliver. She disappeared and appeared so suddenly that the fanatic began using words foreign to his vocabulary like, 'manifest' and 'vanish'. And to Silas and his eagle-eyed snoops, that was a very large blazing red flag.

Something was, indeed, *rotten in Here and Now*.

When all the information was in, Silas flew into one of his rages, "There is only one conclusion to be drawn from all of this—something very un-American, and therefore un-healthy, is definitely going on. *But why haven't you fools gotten to the bottom of it yet?*"

Chapter 52

▼

The VVV installed hidden cameras that never managed to capture Jenny vanishing. The patient snoops' audio tapes did, however, reveal that the subject in question was not always home when she was supposed to be—that is to say, *just after Jenny entered the house.* So, while the outside cameras never caught her going anywhere, the electronic bugs inside picked up no sounds either.

All the vigilantes could do was increase their surveillance.

Silas Malddick had VVV members pose as potential real estate customers—*'Ah, now we'll catch her red handed!'* Silas himself even approached Jenny, with a proposal to establish another development based on the principles of Here and Now—*'Surely I can get something on her when she discusses what makes the development tick!'*

But every effort, including electronic devices hidden in coats, pockets, purses, and attaché cases, brought no incriminating evidence. Except for the fact that the woman sometimes went off the grid, and for lengthy durations—as if she simply *vanished.*

The more mysterious Jenny became, the more sophisticated the VVVs snoop technology became. They used global positioning, infrared sensing devices, and a few gadgets only the CIA knew about. But they still couldn't keep track of this puzzling woman. One of the Vs whispered in frustration, "Is she an *alien?*" And very quietly, since that was against the very thinking of the fanatic Silas.

"If we can't find anything on that Jenny, then *sic the IRS on her,*" shrieked an exasperated Silas. "Follow it up with the FBI—and if they can't find her secret, send in the paparazzi and Hollywood scandal magazines!"

And he continued to rant, "I tell you, Jennifer Oliver is the cause of all these illegitimate conspiracies to mislead and brainwash Mankind that pervade the United States, and the entire free world today! She's concocted this sick 'Ideal Village', and must be exposed! Nothing *real* is ideal, so it's our duty to demonstrate she's an evil fraud. Burn her at the stake—or sue her!"

Of course, Jenny was merely a Leprechaun who happened to have eluded detection at Whereever and Here and Now, and now by Silas Malddick. She was truly *Extraordinary*—to be able to remain in Human form for any length of time proved that.

While she was at the housing development and real estate office, she continued to gather impressions on the *state of Humans,* and dutifully relayed this information to her friends. But, she did need a break every now and then. So, Jenny would dematerialize and vanish—whatever it took to visit Larry, Brian, and her Leprechaun friends.

The Leprechauns barely paid any attention to Jenny's reports—they were so ecstatic in their freedom from Bubbo, the decreased threat from the Humans, and the reinstatement of Brian's *twinkle*. And though Larry himself had vowed to protect Humans after the humiliation of Bubbo, he felt Jenny could handle everything by herself. But, as the Leprechaun-lass showed up more frequently in the Land of the Leprechauns bearing ominous news about Silas and the VVV, Larry could no longer ignore the potential threat.

"'Tis a simple matter," exclaimed Emperor Larry, "if we nip it in the bud. We must set up a perimeter, just as this sinister Silas has. For every Human, we'll assign six Leprechauns. I tell ya', lads and lasses, those brutes won't be able to breathe without us picking up every breath. And if we see them instituting any nefarious actions, we *will* strike before they gain momentum."

And so, the Here and Now Housing Development became the center of two investigations, which soon became three when Jenny picked up on Silas referring his concerns about her to the IRS. The clever lass, however, switched the names and directed the agencies to investigate Silas and his vigilantes instead.

That wasn't the end of it, though—once the IRS became involved, they brought in the FBI and the CIA. Ironically, every agency that Silas wanted to have investigating Here and Now was actually investigating *him*, and the entire situation soon became a comedy of errors.

The federal agencies, sensing there was more to the case than a suspicious fanatic and his group, let Silas do his snooping. *'Why dirty our hands when this fanatic can do the work, and also take the heat if anything goes wrong?'*

Silas and his men entered Jenny's room and searched it thoroughly. They seized books, copied records, and left warnings—but Jenny herself was not harmed. Even after the greatest scrutiny possible, not one thing was found amiss. And because of that, the federal agents finally stepped in—but not the way Silas had hoped.

"Silas Malddick, you are guilty of breaking and entering, and invading a citizen's privacy. You and all your VVV recruits are hereby served with a *Restraining Order*—if you come within one hundred feet of the legal boundaries of the Here and Now development, you will all go to jail. And who knows where after that."

But what good does slapping a mad dog's paw accomplish? Nothing, of course—and so it was with Silas and his underhanded cohorts. They pretended, as it were, to put their tails between their legs and mime, 'I'm sorry, I'll never do it again.' But in the wag of a tail, they were right back to their old tricks.

"Look here," snarled sinister Silas, "there's only one option left. If our government won't take care of them, then we'll have to do it ourselves—go and capture that woman Jenny Oliver!"

Now, being an Extraordinary Leprechaun, Jenny naturally picked up on their intention and relayed it to the Leprechaun leaders. Instantly, Larry, Brian, and all the former Recruiters went into action—that is, they told the hundreds of Leprechauns hovering over Here and Now to *let* the VVV capture Jenny.

"Aye, if the lads want to play tricks, we'll join in the fun!" laughed Larry.

"And all according to our promise," concurred Brian, "for we *are* protecting Johnny and the others when we protect Jenny."

The two then reassured Jenny that the worst that could happen would be a scuffle in a van and some loud talk. "You see, dear, we have a plan of our own."

"I've never complained about spying," said Jenny, "but this rough and tumble stuff—dare I say *violence*—is going a bit far. Isn't there an easier way to put Silas and his scoundrels in their place?"

"Perhaps," answered the sly Leprechaun, "but the way I see it, this is the most certain. When all those initialed agencies pounce on Silas, it'll be ten thousand times worse than when the Grumpys pounced on our Emperor. I tell you Jenny, you've not a thing to worry about—we have everything under control."

"I believe you … aye," said the loyal Jenny. "But when this is over, and if I live through it all, I'll retire on the spot—go to Leprechaun Land and live happily ever after."

"Well said," replied Brian, rising to his Kingly status. "Jenny dear—please wait until after this is finished. You see, we need a tempting bait to catch those rats…."

"*Rat bait*—am I now? And after all I've done for you and the Humans, too!"

"Oh Miss Jenny, you're the sweetest Sprite who ever lived. Your invaluable service deserves an award at least as grand as Larry's—and I'll make certain you get it. Though now's not the time to get fainthearted and retreat. Please lass, let them try to kidnap you. And don't fret—we'll all be in the van with you, and ready to attack if need be."

"Listen to yourself, Brian-the-King—who ever heard of a Leprechaun *attacking?* 'Tis foreign to our very nature. What's happened to you, anyway—have Humans and their density affected you, so that revenge is all you can think about?"

"Not a bit," answered Brian. "We know that sometimes it takes a thorn to remove a thorn, just as de-*twinkling* and humiliating Bubbo was necessary. Remember—and please note, that 'twas the Human who did the physical part. Besides, lass, Larry here vowed to protect the Humans, which means we're all vowed. Please let them do their thing, and we guarantee those vipers will get their own venom."

"You're a most convincing Leprechaun, you are, King Brian."

"Aye—now just how to catch this slimy Silas, so we can settle his case for good."

"I thought you already had a plan!" retorted Jenny.

"Oh, we have one, all right. You see, we let you get kidnapped and relay it to those Human agencies—then they swarm in and do the dirty work. It's all so simple!"

"Sounds good on paper, Brian, but there's a bit of a problem," emphasized Jenny, *twinkling* less than usual.

"And what might that be, lass?"

"I'm not ink on paper."

CHAPTER 53

▼

In the eyes of Leprechauns, *the Taming of Bubbo* was the single greatest act that Man had ever performed for the Leprechaun Race. After all, it saved Leprechaundom itself. But this particular caper promised a new wrinkle—Jenny would be in Larry's shoes—*taking the chance of actually being caught by Humans*—and Humans would be attacking their own.

It was truly an act of faith—could the Leprechauns count on Man to turn on his own kind? Their answer was a unanimous 'yes', since the Imps knew Human aggressiveness well. They just hoped Jenny would not become collateral damage.

While all this was going on, Larry was enjoying his new and well-earned status as Leprechaun Emperor. And enjoy it, he did! Lucy, dear Committed that she was, showered subtle Leprechaun affection on him in private—the kind that Leprechauns never show publicly. Larry was not only honored as the hero he was, but also spoiled since leaving his briar patch.

The new Emperor, however, felt deficient in one area—he felt drawn to Exaltedness. He wanted that high state of development which would allow him to visit Leprechaun Land. For that was the grandest of prizes, the very thing all Leprechauns dreamed about. Being Emperor was one thing, but being *Exalted* was the Pinnacle of Leprechaunhood.

"'Tis a matter of *Being*," said Brian. "There's no way of bringing it on—you know, *making it happen*—any more than there is to faking it. Wanting it is also counter to your very hopes, Larry. The best thing you can do is *forget about it*. When the time is right, and you've achieved the status you wish—in you'll *pop* like the sun on a fine, clear morning. And then, Larry, you will become our Exhalted *Emperor*"

Larry respected the King, so the he engaged himself in Leprechaun busyness. At the moment, the most important thing to do was to take care of Silas and his crew.

What Larry didn't know was that taking the chance of being caught by Humans yet again was, in the eyes of the *Forces on High*, a Grand Act. If the brutes laid hands on him while trying to save Jenny, he might well disappear for all eternity, even though his fellow Leprechauns had elected him their Emperor. So by putting his loyalty on a priority higher than his safety, he was committing the *Ultimate* Leprechaun act.

That did not, indeed, go unnoticed.

One calm and quiet evening just before Jenny's kidnapping, Larry found his vision blurring—and it turned into dizziness. He hadn't felt this disoriented since his first venture into Human denseness. Then, as quick as a wink, he experienced *Pure Clarity*.

No sooner had that happened than Larry visited his dream of dreams, Leprechaun Land.

Exhalted Emperor Larry.

CHAPTER 54

▼

"'Tis Heaven!" said Larry when he faced Brian.

"Indeed," answered the King. "And welcome to Exhalted Leprechaunhood."

"The silence, the perfection … how can anyone do anything destructive after visiting *The Land?*"

"He can't—perfection *is perfection*. And once you've experienced it, you really can do no harm."

Larry's eyes *twinkled* as they had never before, and he cocked his head so far back that his tam-o'-shanter fell off. "Please tell me then, how'd ya' fellas ever get hoodwinked into the Experiment with Bubbo—I mean, how could an Exhalted Leprechaun King ever get tricked? *And how could Bubbo, also an Exhalted One, do such a thing?*"

"Strange as this may sound," replied Brian. "You can answer your own questions by watching Darth Vader in the Human movie *Star Wars.*"

"Hmmm … interesting."

"Indeed—but now, to the present. Silas is to Humans, as Bubbo is to Leprechauns, as Darth is to ... whomever. All apparent thorns—and we know how to handle thorns, we do."

CHAPTER 55

▼

To her fellow Leprechauns, Jenny acted like a Grumpy. On the inside, however, she was overjoyed and looking forward to helping. Moreover, she felt surprisingly strong about saving the Human community. After all, Silas and his vigilantes couldn't do that much harm, could they? On the other hand, they could be very destructive if they went off the deep end.

"Just tell me what you want and I'll do it, *I suppose....*" She dragged out the last words to camouflage her Leprechaun excitement.

So, Jenny Oliver sat on a bench overlooking the playground where Teddy, Colin, Amanda, Samantha, Beebee and Deedee played, while Barbara cuddled little Larry on the opposite bench. Suddenly, four intense men dressed in black leather jackets snatched Jenny up and carried her screaming to a black van. Jenny chose not to fight the men—instead acting totally helpless and meek

When Barbara reached the police on her cell phone, she described one of the villains as having a patch over his left eye, another as having a white streak of hair hanging down his forehead, the third as wearing puffy sideburns, and the fourth as about seven feet tall—all of which the FBI found when Silas' black van was stopped crossing the state line.

Kidnapping is no minor charge, especially when compounded by crossing a state line, and after violating a Restraining Order. When the authorities found a collection of hideous medieval torture tools—thumb screws, bone crushers, ugly things that could shred any part of the Human body, hair pullers, jagged scissors, and numerous piercing and probing skewers—they knew they had their criminals. The van had also been stocked with a spare can of gasoline, a box of matches, a large stake, and pile of very dry wood.

"Weren't you scared, Jenny?" everyone asked when it was over.

"Oh, *of course!* I thought of every worst scenario—that I'd never see Here and Now again, never see you wonderful friends, never be a…. Oh, it was *horrible!*" Jenny knew how to put on a good act when the circumstances required it.

Her friends naturally believed every word she said.

And now, it was all over—both Here and Now and Jenny Oliver were safe.

Jenny was safe and as pretty as ever, as she gazed at her Here and Now friends … knowing that she would not stay much longer. *Within herself, Jenny bubbled and splashed in happiness and gaiety as much as a lively surf on a rocky Scottish shore.*

It took no convincing at all for the jury to pronounce the maximum penalty for Silas Malddick and the entire VVV organization.

CHAPTER 56

▼

After the Great Caper, two things happened to Jenny—she spent less time at Here and Now, and was both happy and sad. Something from the distant past kept forcing its way to the forefront of that beautiful Leprechaun mind—the faintly intriguing scent of something ...

'... *something about the inability of Man and Leprechaun to live together permanently....*'

Though the Humans didn't notice Jenny's inner turmoil, Larry and the Leprechauns did.

"What's going on, lass?" asked Brian. "You're a regular yo-yo, you are—up one minute, down the next. What ails you Jenny dear—now that all's well at Here and Now?"

Emperor Larry answered in Jenny's stead. "Don't probe, my King—I know the cause and 'tis best kept secret, it is."

"A secret only you two hold, by the sounds of it," replied Brian. "Aye, and you've even blocked it out of the telepathy network, so no one else can pick up a thing from your thoughts." After a thoughtful pause, he added, "so it must be one very *big* secret."

"Aye, so it is. But … well.…"

"So it's personal, then?"

"Personal and unusual—most unusual."

"Unusual? Isn't everything about Leprechauns unusual? But it's not for me to meddle in your personal matters, trying to solve your big secret—aye, as long as you two are following the Leprechaun Code, all's well."

"Oh we are, Brian—to be sure. There are, of course, some codes obvious to the eye … while others are harder to fathom, because they're in small print—don't ya' see."

"I do and I don't. My feeling is that I'll never learn your secret—but then, maybe.…"

CHAPTER 57

▼

It took some time for things to settle down in Leprechaun-dom, and Here and Now. So much had happened in such a short span of time. Even so, a great deal had been learned during this whirlwind of activity.

Normally, Leprechauns exist for millennia with virtually nothing happening. And Humans ... well, catastrophes did occur more frequently. Had Larry Leprechaun kept his own Journal, he would certainly have recorded these events:

The Highlanders
Bubbo's Vengeful Thinking
The Experiment
The Grand Tour and Intermissions
Human Grumpys Escape Whereever
My Capture and Humiliation by Johnny
Bubbo Stealing the Exalteds' *Twinkles*
The Taming of Bubbo
Becoming Emperor
The Birth of Little Larry
Sean and Sarah Lowrey Exposed

Silas Malddick's Investigation
Jenny Oliver Kidnapped
VVV Caught and Jailed
My Exalted Experience of Leprechaun Land

CHAPTER 58

▼

Leprechaun life returned to normal—there were no conflicts, no one dominated anyone else, and there were no invasions from the outside. Bubbo had been stripped of his powers, and no Exalted was threatened.

The only oddity was Jenny Oliver—she resided mostly at Here and Now, though no one knew why. Spying was certainly no longer needed, since the Humans and Leprechauns had smoothed out the relationship between their Races. Jenny's presence was pleasant, and no Human knew her true identity. On the other hand, her growing discomfort, both surface and subtle, suggested that it was merely a matter of time before she moved back home to Leprechaun Land. Meanwhile, she certainly added charm wherever she was.

Midge, who was habituated to doing vanishing exercises every morning, finally stopped the drill. Everyone felt that it sent mixed messages, especially to Teddy, Colin, Amanda, Samantha, Beebee and Deedee—as well as to little Larry—for no one else walked around half here and partly there.

Barry and Pam Clarke bought two more homes from McMann Realty as investment properties to be rented. They also invested in the developments we had established in other communities. And Barry was still curious about the whereabouts of the fellow in the tweed suit and cocky tam-o'-shanter.

Johnny's faithful secretary, Sheila, got married. And because she liked her job so much, she remained with McMann Realty. Her husband, Dexter, shot pool with Glenn, Ben, Stan, and me every Wednesday while our respective wives had tea and coffee, and gossiped.

Tammy Taylor—Barbara's close friend and Maid of Honor, felt drawn to Here and Now more and more. At one time, she even thought of asking if she could move in, but didn't for some inexplicable reason. It was enough to visit and watch her friend handle the home school so naturally.

One day, a strange event occurred. Everyone was convinced that it could only have happened once *everything* had been settled between Leprechauns and Humans. The residents of Here and Now had gathered in their large Community Center, when as suddenly as flicking a switch, up *popped* an oddly dressed group of individuals.

One wore Austrian shorts, another was in Nepalese garb, a third wore nothing but a loin cloth, two wore polar bear parkas, one was topped with a sombrero, and a very aboriginal-looking figure with curly hair sported a bone in his nose. The group was rounded out by the familiar and ruddy face of Larry Leprechaun, dressed as always—but with one exception.

On this occasion, he also wore something on his face—his own full-grown, bright orange beard. And along with these former Recruiters was the most rag-a-muffin, down-at-the-mouth, beardless Leprechaun anyone had ever seen.

Larry announced boldly, "Friends all—Glenn Mye rhymes-with-eye, Ben Bow rhymes-with-yo, Stan Lew rhymes-with-you; and you too, Johnny McMann rhymes-with-pan. Seeing as we've all been through a great deal together, my friends thought 'twould be fitting if we brought—as ya' Humans say—closure to everything."

"Now don't ya' get yer Grumpy dandruff up. Ye'd be interested to know that we Leprechauns were fooled as completely as yerselves, and all by this fella here known as Bubbo, who you've met briefly before. That's right folks, 'twas he who dreamed up the whole scheme—that is, the Experiment. But no matter, since we now have him in tow, and all wounds have healed. Aye, that's the very reason we're here now."

Emperor Larry waved the spunkless rag-a-muffin bundle called Bubbo into the shadows behind the crowd.

"Now, while I was part of the North American Whereever, others held the fort in other spots. I dare say, you've heard about them all, but not yet met them. Well, here they are." He introduced them one by one. "Here is Bascomb from Vienna—now aren't those the grandest shorts you've ever seen? And here's Lung Chu from Nepal—I'll wager ya' don't see the likes of this garb at Here and Now. This is Pauul from the Congo—sporty outfit, eh? And Julio from South America—quite a stylish sombrero there. Here we have Sidje from the North Pole—and that's authentic Polar Bear, friends. Say hello over here to Ooma from the South Pole—ever wonder what they wear there? And finally, here's Brian the King from the Australian Outback—and 'tis the prize winning nose-bone of all, I'm sure. Recruiters they were—and all fine Leprechaun Leaders to boot."

Barbara held little Larry higher, so he could see everyone.

"So, dear, these are the ones you visited on your Grand Tour, while I stayed in the Village?" Barbara asked me excitedly. "Hmmm ... Yes ... you did describe them well in your Journal."

"They're the very ones," I replied, happy to see the Recruiters again. "Though I never expected to see them again, much less in a Human dwelling."

"No matter," said Emperor Larry, whose *tam* had become more a crown than cap. "We've come to grips with our fear of Humans, and realize 'tis only in a dire emergency that ya' become violent. That may not be true with others of yer Race, but it certainly is with all of ya' here, aye."

"It is," I admitted, speaking for all of my Human friends, "though I think that Mike McGee and the others would amend what you've said. It's not that we *become* violent, but rather that we go into action and do what it takes to set things straight—and I'm sure that appears violent to you sensitive folks."

The residents of Here and Now all nodded in agreement.

"'Tis all in how ya' look at it—wouldn't ya' say?" concluded Larry. "But, no matter—we're all here to show that we harbor no ill feelings. And to prove our good will, we hereby—each and every one of us—offer ya' our hands in friendship. For we trust y'all, we do—and no longer fear further entrapment or densification."

"And we no longer fear you tricking us or working to undermine the Human Race," I declared. "And perhaps, some day, our *Developed Humans* … ahem.… Well, anyway—perhaps we shall work together closely again in the future."

There was hearty laughter, joyful greetings, happy hand clasps, and back-slapping that made the rafters of the Community Center rattle. This was followed by the closest experience a Human can have to a Leprechaun Gathering.

The great reconciliation was complete.

CHAPTER 59

▼

Long, long ago in a Village named John O'Groats at the tip of the Scottish Highlands, a beautiful Leprechaun watched the surf dance about the rocky shore.

"What ails ya', lass?" asked her male friend.

The wind whistled through her hair, highlighting her natural charm. "'Tis a lad I met in my mind, but can never have," she moaned, sobbing into her folded arms.

"Now, now, lass. 'Tis no way for a Leprechaun to be acting. But tell me why ya' cannot have the love of yer heart. Maybe I can help. Aye, they don't call me Extraordinary for nothing."

"Well, my friend," she replied, "I don't see that it matters, because I can never have him. He's one of them—you know, a *Man*."

"Aye, 'tis no wonder you're so mournful, my dear! But you're not in as bad a predicament as ya' think."

"Why's that, now? Everyone knows Man and Leprechaun can never marry."

"To be sure. Aye ... but I'm remembering something from ancient times, I am. Hmmm ... *what is it, that bit o'ancient lore....*"

After a lengthy pause, he exclaimed, "Aha ... yesss, lass. I do believe there's a way."

"*A way, you say?*" she replied, her tears stopping and her face beaming like the sun itself. "Oh, do tell me at once. How can I unite with the Man of my longing?"

"'Tis a way, 'tis a way...."

"Quit torturing me now—you must tell me before I throw myself into the very sea."

"Yer threat's idle, m'dear, and ya' know it. Leprechauns live through all eternity. But I'll tell ya' anyway, for I can't stand to see one so beautiful in the same pain I feel. Ye' see, I suffer from the very same malady."

"You *do?*" asked the lass, brushing wind-swept hair from her face. "Then why aren't you using this *Grand Secret* yourself? Is this all blarney—and you're merely teasing me now?"

"Truth is, lass, I'd as good as forgotten it since my heart's been aching for so long. Aye, 'til ya' reminded me this very moment. But do give me a moment, and I'll see if I can't recall the particulars."

The pensive pause was electric.

"Mmm ... hmm.... *Yes, quite!*"

"And ya' know what, dear?" he announced triumphantly. "If ya' like, I think we can solve this heartache together for our respective loves."

"'Twould be grand indeed! You're *sure* now—for I don't want my heart set, only to be let down … You're *certain* that we can both have our beloved Humans in the future?"

"Aye, and since ya' seem so sincere, I'll tell ya' the technique outright. Yer heart-most desire will come by great craving, untold wishing, and eternal yearning. Aye, 'til you're almost green in the face. And by such craving, wishing, and yearning, the Powers Above will allow ya' to give birth to a Human child. But there is a great price to be paid. Sadly, we can't marry our beloved, though we *can* bear their young."

"Seems like a price beyond belief. Nevertheless my friend, you've given me hope. Yes, I'll crave, wish, and yearn for all eternity if need be. For even one single moment of his love will be worth it. And bearin' his child will be Heaven."

The Extraordinary Leprechaun sat in silence as the surf danced merrily against the rocky shore.

'Aye, 'twill be my very Mission.'

Many years later, Jenny Oliver became a mother to a bouncy little lad she named *'Johnny'*.

CHAPTER 60

▼

Groggy from a long day's work, I lay sprawled on the sofa. I had been reading the last year's entries in the Larry Log, and would have paid more attention to Little Larry, had tiredness not overtaken me.

In that half-awake, half-sleep mode, my mind churned—*'Why didn't Barb go with me on the Grand Tour? Where was Larry during this time? Why John O'Groats? And where's Jenny now?'*

Little Larry climbed onto my chest and mumbled, "Goo-goo gaa-gaa." His stubby fingers poked at the Journal, and seeing the name 'Larry', the *twinkle-eyed* little fella said, *"Da-da."*

As he slid off my chest, I heard Barb coo, "it's all right dear—Mommy will catch you."

The End

978-0-595-45400-6
0-595-45400-3

Printed in the United States
97525LV00001B/1-99/A